THE CHAOS OF CHUNG-FU
And Other Stories

It is in a litter-strewn back alley in downtown Chicago that private investigator Jack Murphy first spies the poster. Damp and tattered, it looks like something from a hundred years ago: THE SORCERY OF CHUNG-FU, *An Evening of Oriental Magic and Mystery*. But Murphy gets more than he bargains for when his investigation of a back-street Chinese magician over suspicions of kidnapping becomes a terrifying fight for his life. This and four other tales of the sinister, supernatural and macabre make this a truly chilling collection . . .

EDMUND GLASBY

THE CHAOS OF CHUNG-FU

And Other Stories

Complete and Unabridged

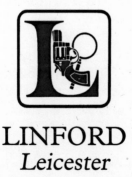

LINFORD
Leicester

First published in Great Britain in 2013

First Linford Edition
published 2014

A catalogue record for this book is available
from the British Library.

ISBN 978–1–4448–2121–5

Published by
F. A. Thorpe (Publishing)
Anstey, Leicestershire

Set by Words & Graphics Ltd.
Anstey, Leicestershire
Printed and bound in Great Britain by
T. J. International Ltd., Padstow, Cornwall

This book is printed on acid-free paper

The Chaos of Chung-Fu

Jack Murphy's investigations into the disappearances were to lead him into a shadowy and dangerous world of Oriental horror, sorcery and madness.

It was in a litter-strewn back alley in downtown Chicago that private investigator Jack Murphy first saw the poster. Damp and tattered, pinned to the wall of a squalid Chinese takeaway, it looked like something from a hundred years ago.

The evening was quite dark and it was raining heavily. Water ran from the brim of his hat and he pulled up the collar of his long coat before crossing over to take a closer look.

He flicked his torch on and shone the beam directly at the poster, grimacing somewhat at what he saw. For the poster was a flyer, an advertisement for a forthcoming theatrical event and one which, judging by the images depicted, was not for the faint of heart.

Emblazoned along the top, in stark, slanting lettering was:

THE SORCERY OF CHUNG-FU
An Evening of Oriental Magic and Mystery

Chung-Fu. Now there was a name he had heard whispered on the streets.

The image that dominated the garish poster was of a sly-looking Chinese man with a tasselled skullcap and an expensive, embroidered silk robe. Below him were a series of alarming, theatrical scaled-down drawings: a scantily-clad woman shown in mid-scream, strapped to a rack as a pendulum blade swung low; a grinning, hideous puppet-like thing, its dagger held aloft; a man cowering from two tigers and, in the bottom left corner, another man, open-mouthed, vomiting a stream of spiders. Columns around which massive pythons coiled, bordered the central theme.

There was a bizarreness to it that unnerved even him, filled him with an uneasy sensation, which sent a shiver through his body. Whether there was any connection between it and the rash of disappearances in this area that he was investigating he didn't know, but as he had so little to go on, it was a line of enquiry he would keep open.

From the details he had managed to piece together, the disappearances had been happening for several years and there were some common features that made him think that there was definitely something sinister behind them. All of the missing were lowlifes; those social unfortunates that the police were not overly concerned with; the downtrodden demimonde — vagrants, ladies of easy virtue and drunks for the main part. And, had it not been for the disappearance of Harry 'Two-Bellies' Lafayette — a local gangster with high-up friends, he doubted whether anyone would have bothered to investigate at all.

Murphy found himself reflecting on this as he studied the poster. There was a forthcoming show scheduled for a week's time and, after confirming the venue, he decided it was a show he was going to attend. That being the case, he thought it prudent to see what, if anything, he could discover about this enigmatic Chinese showman and his magic show.

'Big' Teddy Maxwell, the head of the local mob, afraid that a gang war might be starting on his turf, was paying him good money and he wanted results. As things currently stood he had no other avenues of investigation, everything so far turning out to be dead ends.

Removing the poster from the wall, Murphy rolled it up and stuck it into an inside coat pocket. The rain was becoming heavier, drenching him in its miserable deluge. He stepped closer to the wall and reached for a cigarette, lighting it with a deft flick of a match. He inhaled, taking the smoke into his lungs before exhaling a cloud of blue smoke from his nostrils.

Some inner intuition, one that he had learned to trust over his years as a private investigator, told him that there was something highly suspect about this Chung-Fu, something that definitely warranted deeper investigation. Just what it was, well that was something he hoped to discover.

With that thought, he hunched his shoulders and stalked, broodingly, back to his apartment, completely unaware of the pair of dark eyes that watched his every movement, tracking him with an intensity of purpose.

* * *

It was the sound of the creak of the seventh tread on the stairs that made Murphy look up from where he sat at the table, on which his half-empty bottle of cheap whisky rested. The sound of a careless footfall.

Immediately, he got up and sidestepped to his right, towards where his coat, and more importantly, his holstered gun lay. He was halfway there when the door burst open and an Oriental-looking thug rushed in, a knife in his hand. Clearly this was something other than a social visit.

The knife came flying and Murphy ducked so that it went clear of his head and juddered into the far wall. He fumbled for his gun but the man launched a spinning kick that caught him high in the chest, knocking the air from him and sending him back. Toppling over a chair, he just had time to roll aside to avoid another savage kick.

Scrambling to his feet, Murphy raised his fists. A self-trained pugilist, he adopted a defensive stance, ready and more than willing to give his attacker what for. The man came forward, making a series of vicious swings, his piggy, close-set eyes filled with hatred.

He came at a rush. Murphy saw his arm go back as he made to bring down a chop with the side of his right hand. Shifting nimbly to the side, Murphy blocked the attack, biting back the agony in his arm. He then wrong-footed his attacker, grabbed him and, using his raw strength, swung him back towards the door.

There was a cry of pain as the two collided. The private investigator sprang forward, delivering a solid right hook to the unfortunate's back. He briefly considered getting his gun. He was just about to, when the man sprang to his feet with the agility of a wild cat and leapt forward in an acrobatic move that took him by surprise. He tried to block the sudden flurry of kicks that struck him, forcing him backs. The back of his legs struck the table. Reaching out with his right hand, he made a grab for the whisky bottle. Swinging it down, he crashed it over the man's head. Glass shattered.

Dazed and hurt, the Chinese man shook his head, trying to refocus. He recovered quickly and came at Murphy again, his hands weaving in deft movements before him.

And then there were hands at Murphy's throat, ragged nails biting into the flesh at his neck. Fighting back the hurt, he jabbed a clenched fist into the man's stomach, making him release his hold.

Uttering a curse, the thug staggered back, falling to his knees under the force of the punch. A tough and wiry opponent, he lunged forward, arms flailing, head down, pummelling into Murphy as he pushed himself upright, catching him before he could dispatch him with a hefty kick. Together they crashed back, colliding with a chest of drawers and falling to the floor.

Scrambling to his feet, Murphy grabbed his attacker by his shirt collar. He himself was then smacked in the stomach. There was a dull roaring in his ears and all of the wind seemed to rush from his lungs. A follow-up chop sent Murphy reeling back against the window, his head temporarily swimming. Like striking snakes, more blows blurred before his eyes; swings and jabs that he had trouble countering.

Murphy's ribs and stomach ached and things were now getting desperate. He would have to resort to a bit of dirty fighting, the style he had learnt on the mean streets of Brooklyn where he had been raised. Catching hold of one of the man's arms, he hauled him close, his other hand reaching out and grabbing a handful of unwashed, greasy hair. He pulled violently, ripping hair from his assailant's scalp, before bringing the head down to meet his rising knee.

Howling in agony, the man tried to break free, smacking two quick-fire jabs into Murphy's ribs. Murphy held on, hauled his attacker to his feet, spun him around and drove him, headfirst, into the wall. Grabbing his stunned foe by the back of his collar, he repeated the act twice more before throwing the badly battered man to the floor. He was just about to finish him off with a savage kick when, to his surprise, he got to his feet.

Snarling his anger, Murphy grabbed him in a headlock. Applying all of his strength, he hoped to squeeze the life from him or break his neck.

Like a slimy eel, the other wriggled free, nipped behind Murphy and hacked two chops into his kidneys. Groaning his hurt, Murphy half-fell and reeled across the room out into the corridor. Warped and bleary images dashed across his vision. He shook his head and tried to focus. Suddenly a chair came flying. He braced himself as it cracked off his right shoulder. The force of the smash almost sent him careering down the narrow stairs.

Murphy's implacable enemy somersaulted forward, landing nimbly on his feet.

Wiping away the blood that ran from a split lower lip, Murphy landed several solid blows with his right fist. He then dodged past the other, nipped back into his room and made a frantic attempt to get his gun. His attacker sprang on his back and the two of them made a bizarre shadow outline on the wall as they fought and grappled. Murphy tried to throw the other clear. More by accident than design he stumbled and, using his raw strength, he hauled the man free, dashing him head over heels out through his apartment window. Glass shattered.

The Chinese man fell past the fire escape and plummeted five storeys to the dingy street below.

Murphy looked down and saw the body, illuminated in the flashing red neon light of the late-night diner nearby.

Then, before his disbelieving eyes, something truly unexpected happened. The body lying broken on the rain-washed street below exploded in a firecracker burst of streamers, flame and smoke! The acrid smell of gunpowder wafted up from some fifty feet below.

* * *

'Big' Teddy Maxwell was lots of things, but he certainly wasn't big — at least not in the physical sense. He was short and balding, clean-shaven and debonair, but there was a glint of menace in his eyes as he glared at Murphy. 'What do you mean, he just turned to smoke?'

Murphy stood his ground. He was used to dealing with wise guys, having spent much of his life in the company of bootleggers and racketeers. 'I'm telling you, that's what happened. I threw him from my apartment window and then he just sort of blew up, like a dummy filled with fireworks on the pavement. By the time I got down there to check, there was nothing left but a pile of streamers and that smell you get after someone's pulled a Christmas cracker.'

'Well I'm not paying you good money to go round fighting things that ain't real. I want you to find out what's happened to 'Two-Bellies', you hear me?' Maxwell turned to one of his goons who stood behind him: a thick-set ape of a man with a black handlebar moustache and a squint. 'You ever heard of any of this rubbish, 'Muscles'?'

'No, boss.' 'Muscles' shook his head

'You've got to believe me,' said

Murphy. 'I don't understand it. The only thing I can think is that there's some connection with this Chung-Fu guy. Maybe it was some kind of fakery; Chinese magic. I don't know. Anyhow, I've been lying low just in case someone's got it in for me. Could be this Chung-Fu thinks I'm on to him.'

'Chung-Fu's nothing but a two-bit pain in the ass. He thinks he rules Chinatown but he can't even run a laundry business. This magic show, I bet that's just a load of baloney to try and bring in a bit of extra dough.' Maxwell cracked his knuckles. 'Still, I think you should keep an eye on him. Last thing I need right now, what with those boys down in the south giving me grief, is for that damned slant to muscle in on our operations here. If he is holding 'Two-Bellies' then he may try and get some information out of him. But me and 'The Bellies' go way back and I know he won't squeal.'

'So what do you want me to do?' asked Murphy.

'I want you to do what I'm paying you to do. Find 'Two-Bellies'. If you think that yellow son of a bitch is involved then find out and tell me.'

'Okay. I'll see what this show's all about,' Murphy replied, 'but I might need a bit of support if things turn nasty.'

'Don't tell me you need one of my men to hold you by the hand? It's only a freakin' circus show.'

'Yeah, but you didn't get beat up by a dummy filled with Chinese firecrackers, did you?'

Disgruntled, Maxwell shook his head. 'I'll see if I can spare anyone. Now go, go watch the clowns.' He reached into a pocket and removed a dollar bill. 'Here, the candy floss is on me.'

'Muscles' and some of the others chuckled.

* * *

Chung-Fu. The mere name had come to instill a certain terror in Murphy that now brought gooseflesh to his skin. And yet, here he now stood, waiting in line with the forty or so others in the pouring rain outside the ramshackle theatre. There

13

were many more posters stuck to the walls, identical to the one he had first seen a week ago.

The crowd shuffled forward a step, then another; a sign that the doors had opened. Swallowing a lump in his throat, Murphy moved forward, eyes scrutinising the sinister face of the Chinese magician. He sneered at it in an act of bravado and scratched the stubble on his chin. If he were the one responsible for the disappearances and if it had been he who had sent that strange assassin after him, there was going to be hell to pay. He would have to be a damned good magician to avoid six slugs shot at close range. That was his intent, to catch him backstage and interrogate him after the show was over.

The entrance to the theatre had been done up rather tackily to resemble some kind of Chinese temple, with dragons and red and gold banners hung here and there. It looked cheap and uninspiring and it was of no surprise to Murphy that many, if not all, of those in the queue were tramps, winos and deadbeats. A pervasive air of sordidness prevailed, the smell from those waiting to go in adding to its overall unpleasantness.

Still, Murphy had frequented worse dens of iniquity.

From the talk he overheard whilst waiting to enter it became apparent that none had ever been to one of Chung-Fu's performances before.

Murphy bought a ticket from the coolie hat-wearing usher on duty, paid a nickel for a bag of peanuts at the makeshift kiosk and was directed to one of the doors through which the crowd was already filing. Now in the foyer, it seemed that everywhere he looked he saw more posters, some depicting forthcoming attractions, others highlighting stages of Chung-Fu's none-too-illustrious career.

It was dark in the theatre.

Murphy found his place, about halfway down the decrepit fleapit. He settled into his uncomfortable seat, his sight virtually useless in the shadowy gloom. He ate a handful of nuts. Figures shifted in the darkness around him as others took their places.

Minutes passed, the constant murmuring of those around increasing the sense of trepidation that was slowly giving way to fear within his mind. His body felt stiff and cold. A tiny muscle in his cheek twitched uncontrollably. He felt as though the theatre had become filled with amorphous, muttering things, each hungry for his blood.

Then the music started. To call it music would be an over statement, for this was a dreadful clanging clamour mixed with tinkling bells, clashing gongs and beating drums; an infernal, diabolical din that grew from silence into a hideous cacophony. Thankfully it faded, only to be replaced with a mournful, dirge-like singing that seemed to rise like something dead and wailing from the theatre basement, where all manner of things could lurk. Like a dark, unseen tide, it quickly drowned out the hubbub from those seated.

Murphy patted the lump of his gun, thankful that he had it.

Spotlights illuminated the stage. A thick, red, moth-eaten curtain concealed whatever lay beyond. The music stopped.

Then came a voice, a strange ethereal voice reciting strange Chinese words that Murphy couldn't understand. Accompanying this incomprehensible introduction came a shuffling, crooked figure from the right side of the stage. It was an ancient man with a long, wispy grey beard. He was dressed in a rough grey-brown cloak, a knobbly stick in his hand. His movements were arthritic and doddery and, nearing the centre, he stumbled and nearly fell over.

Some in the audience laughed.

The Chinese commentary stopped.

Murphy squinted. Was this Chung-Fu in disguise?

The old man raised his terribly wrinkled face. 'Good evening and welcome.' His voice was wavering. 'May I take this opportunity to thank you all for coming on such a miserable night. We have a host of entertainers this evening. Tonight's first act features those manic midgets from Old Shanghai — Sammy Hung and his sons: Ling, Jing, Xing and Weng. Then we have, all the way from the Grand Guignol theatre in Paris, France,

17

Monsieur Claude Giraudin. After his performance, you're sure to be enthralled by the puppetry of Huey Labada.'

Huey Labada. Murphy sat up. He thought he had heard that name before somewhere but for the life of him he couldn't remember where.

'Tonight's penultimate act before the main attraction is Madame Li Sung, the Empress of Escapology. And then, the one you've all come to see, the Master of the Macabre, the Chinese Conjuror, the Devil of Xiang-Shang-Po, *Chung-Fu*!'

With no further words, he shambled off the stage.

The curtain rose, albeit clumsily. The backdrop was a poor mock-up of a dusty Chinese village street, dilapidated, ramshackle timber houses with red and gold banners hanging from windows and doorways. A large cart filled with marrows and pumpkins rested to one side.

For a time nothing happened and the murmuring in the crowd grew. Then, with the crack and bang of numerous fireworks a small Chinese dragon scurried out onto the stage, the feet of its operators clearly

18

visible. It was a crude-looking thing of scarlet and gold, adorned with streamers, its head shaggy, its large goggle eyes wobbling, its mouth snapping. It weaved and danced for a few minutes before snaking off stage.

A moment later five midgets rushed out. The diminutive quintet cavorted, performing acts of none-too-great dexterity. With a hoot and a cry the entertainers leapt, somersaulted and cartwheeled. One walked on his hands, presenting his fat backside to the audience. Clambering together, they then formed a human pyramid; a bizarre, fleshy effigy that held for a few seconds before toppling over.

A huge roar of laughter came from the spectators.

After this display of their acrobatic abilities three of them ran off stage and returned with huge guan daos — vicious-looking Chinese polearms — with which they fought one another, their attacks and parries poorly rehearsed. The other two produced hand axes with which they started to juggle. Every so often one of them would fall over or mistime a catch, often with bloody results. They would get a laugh all the same.

And then, seemingly over before it had started, Sammy Hung and his sons linked hands and bowed in unison.

'Let's hear your appreciation.' The aged compere shuffled from the wings, clapping as he came. 'Weren't they great?'

'Utter rubbish!' shouted a tramp in the second row. 'Pathetic!' He stood up and began making rude gestures at the entertainers.

Murphy glanced over, a wry smile on his lips. He agreed with the heckler's sentiments, but —

Suddenly the lead midget rushed forward brandishing one of the hand axes. He looked around, his eyes wild, popping from his head. 'What that you say?' he screeched.

Murphy stared dumbstruck as the crazed dwarf ranted on.

'You want this? You want this between ears?'

'I dare you, you damned — '

The hurled hatchet spun and flashed end over end, thudding with a meaty thwack into the heckler's right shoulder. Screaming his agony to the ceiling, the unfortunate then began to push his way to the aisle. With blood oozing from where the hatchet lay embedded, the man stumbled to the end of the row when a second hand axe struck with deadly accuracy into the side of his head. The force of the blow catapulted him over and into the next row where he fell upended. His legs twitched for a moment before the body slumped down into the space between the seats.

There followed a stunned silence, a silence that was soon interrupted by the sound of the angry midget and his sons cursing and stomping off stage.

The curtain fell. Two stagehands rushed out with a stretcher and took the body away.

Murphy sat, like the majority of the onlookers, shocked and horrified at what had just happened. *Good God!* What kind of barbarism was this? Or could it just have been no more than a well-staged illusion; a part of the act? His thoughts seemed to be echoed by some in the audience as a ripple of uneasy laughter spread across the chamber. He watched as others left their seats, moving to the side aisles, either fearful that Sammy Hung would return and vent his wrath on them or else in readiness to leave.

The doddery old man returned. 'Well, that was something else, I'm sure you'd all agree. As for tonight's second act, we are truly honoured to have with us an undisputed master of illusion. May I present, the *one*, *the only* . . . *Monsieur . . . Claude Giraudin*!'

The lights dimmed.

The curtain rose.

The haunting organ groaning of Bach's 'Toccata and Fugue in D Minor' started up as clouds of dry ice billowed across the stage.

Murphy could see that the stage had been transformed into an eerie, moon-lit, cemetery-like setting: hastily-put-up headstones, an old plastic tree and a spike railing. In the middle, he could discern a caped organist with a top hat, his back to the audience, a large ornate church-organ before him.

The playing stopped and the seated figure turned around.

Thoroughly grotesque — his hair patchy and straggly, his face sunken and cadaverous — he bore more than a passing resemblance to Lon Chaney senior's portrayal of the Phantom of the Opera.

Removing his top hat with the flair of a true showman, Giraudin then walked over to one of the headstones. Like a graveyard ghoul, he perched atop it and stared out into the crowd, his long, spindly legs stretched out before him.

Murphy didn't like what he saw. He gulped. This whole performance was becoming too strange for him. He thought he had mentally prepared himself for some degree of oddness but this was surpassing anything he had ever seen before.

On stage, Giraudin rose to his feet and passed his hand over his top hat with a flourish. With a wiggle of his fingers, he plunged his arm inside and pulled out not a white rabbit *but a severed head!* It was that of one of the Hung brothers!

A loud cry of horror went through the auditorium.

Murphy's heart lurched inside his chest and the man on his right vomited.

Giraudin grinned, his face like a skull. He looked at the head before throwing it into the crowd. With a blue flash, it vanished in mid-flight, drawing another cry from the spectators.

So it was just an illusion. Murphy settled a little. No doubt papier mâché duplicates filled with fireworks. He was disgusted, but impressed. This sure beat the petty card tricks and the 'find the lady' that was known to win a buck or two by fooling drunks in the bars around town.

A second midget's head, a third and a fourth were also removed from the hat. Giraudin studied each, at one point lovingly caressing one's cheek, before throwing it to the audience. They all vanished as had the first. He turned and walked to the opposite end of the stage. Hat held in one hand, he raised his other arm before sticking it inside. This time he screamed; his face a portrait in pain. He pulled his arm free. Clamped on to his hand, its teeth around his wrist, was Sammy Hung's head!

As one, the spectators screamed. Some, deciding they had seen enough, made for the exit.

Hiraudin added to the screaming. Desperately, he tried to shake Sammy's head free. The head fell back into the hat, which now lay on the floor, dragging the Frenchman with it.

Captivated by the scene before him, Murphy watched as the top hat slowly began to swallow Giraudin. This couldn't be happening, his rational brain tried to tell him. It was magic of such a high calibre that it defied explanation. But that was all it was — a clever magic trick, performed by means unknown in order to befuddle and entertain the masses. This was something that he had never experienced before. He had always disbelieved in the reality of magic, in anything remotely supernatural — it had no place in his hard-bitten, well-ordered life. He dealt only with things that he could see, feel, talk to and, if necessary, shoot. Now, his mind floundered frenziedly, out of its depth, groping for something firm and sane on which it could anchor itself. *Was it a trick?* Some part of his mind demanded an answer.

Giraudin's limbs danced in spasmodic judders as, like a constrictor snake with its prey, the hat began to expand as it drew him in. Blood poured over the brim. With a slurping noise, the stage magician was engulfed from head to waist. Somehow, he staggered to his feet, blood covering what remained visible of him — his lower half. He crashed against one of the headstones and fell to the floor.

Grimly, Murphy watched as Giraudin's legs kicked as though he was trying to right himself once more.

Suddenly, with a nauseating slurp, the hat devoured everything bar one foot. A trouser leg and a well-polished shoe protruded at an odd angle.

Spotlights fell on the bloodstained hat. It sat alone on the stage, steaming and burping like some gorged, fat toad.

A disturbing minute passed.

Murphy stared, confused, dumbstruck

and utterly disgusted.

Then it happened. Like a geyser, a torrent of blood and guts fountained out of the hat. The crowd screamed in shock and revulsion. Still the red spray came, covering the stage in its gory, lumpy soup. Had anyone been left in the front row they would have been drenched.

The top hat rested on the stage, Giraudin's unmoving foot defying Murphy's sense of reality. He had hoped it would move, disappear, do something, anything but lie there. If it had gone, he could have rationalised that there had been some hidden trapdoor or other concealed exit — some escape hatch into which the entertainer had gone.

Matters were made worse when a stagehand in a coolie hat rushed on and lifted the hat, foot and all, off the floor before scampering away again.

A disgruntled- looking man with a mop and bucket came on stage. Muttering darkly to himself, he began cleaning up the copious blood spill.

The lights dimmed and the curtain fell. This had to be fake, Murphy told himself. It had to be. He had read in the papers about some of these shock-horror grisly shows. They were rated not by talent but on gore content; the bloodier the better. In some ways he supposed it was like the old Roman arenas — the crowd baying for blood. It made him sick but he had to remain focused. Maxwell was getting edgy and unless he found out something soon about 'Two-Bellies' then Murphy's own life could be in danger.

A spotlight fell on the stage, following the movements of the wizened host. 'Well, that was something to tell the grand-children about, wouldn't you say? May I present this evening's next act, *Huey Labada*!' He began clapping in a doomed attempt to get the crowd to do likewise before retreating off stage.

The curtain rose.

A man in a pin-striped jacket looking every bit an archetypal mobster stood on the stage. In his left hand he held a Thompson submachine gun. Cradled in his right arm was something from a child's nightmare. The thing was lumpy and potato-shaped. What face it had resembled a cross between a battered child and a drooling bulldog. It was dressed in an old-fashioned convict outfit complete with arrow-striped markings, a cap, and a ball and chain manacled around one ankle. Whereas most of the body looked stunted and deformed, its arms looked like human arms and moved accordingly.

The theatrical backdrop was of a dimly-lit Chicago street. Sound effects included the wail of a police car in the distance.

'Alright you guys,' said the ventriloquist. 'Listen up. I'm Huey Labada.'

'An' I'm his sidekick, 'Two-Bellies',' said the dummy.

Murphy's heart skipped a beat. He stared hard, trying to discern the dummy's features. Was it just his imagination or was there a vague resemblance between it and the photograph Maxwell had given him of the missing 'Two-Bellies'? But how could that be possible? This grotesque thing was no larger than a five-year-old child.

'We've got a great show for you folks tonight,' said Labada.

'Have we?' asked 'Two-Bellies'.

'Sure have. But first we're gonna take

care of that mug who works in the jewellery shop. The one who set you up and put you in the slammer.'

There ensued a long drawn-out theatrical scene that involved Labada and his 'dummy' in a mock hold-up of a jeweller's, the part of the shop owner being played by the little old man who had introduced all of the acts so far. The lights then dimmed and the backdrop altered, so that the images of shadow-puppets could be projected on to it. Whether this was done by cast members off stage or via some form of cinematography, it was hard for Murphy to discern. It was impressive nonetheless and although not a Broadway production, the scale of it took him completely by surprise.

However, like all of the previous acts it ended tragically and bloodily. For, in the final scene, Labada and 'Two-Bellies' were cornered by the police, the latter depicted through a combination of real actors and more shadow puppetry. There ensued a ferocious gun-battle, the sounds of the pyrotechnics and special effects deafening.

Riddled with bullets, Labada staggered dramatically to the front of the stage and collapsed in a pool of blood, landing atop the deformed dummy-thing.

Labada's demise was followed by some hesitant applause, although by now the theatre had emptied somewhat, many individuals having seen enough.

Once more the curtain descended.

A riot of crazy notions swam darkly in Murphy's mind. There was a feeling of sick apprehension in the pit of his stomach. His brain heaved and twisted with something he was unable to fully control or understand as though something was tugging at his sanity. He doubted whether he could watch much more of this bizarre horror show. And then there had been that thing, *'Two-Bellies'*. It surely wasn't coincidental — however, was it the link he needed?

The old man returned. 'And now for Madame Li Sung.'

The drapes were lifted, revealing a tranquil temple garden scene: fountains, topiary-styled hedgerows and a distant pagoda. Faint chimes tinkled.

31

An exotic, tattooed Chinese woman in a purple silk kimono descended gracefully from the ceiling on invisible wires. At least Murphy assumed there were invisible wires. A stagehand then wheeled out a large cabinet, assisting the woman inside before padlocking it, turning it around to show there was no apparent means of escape at the rear. Then, with a puff of smoke, she reappeared at the opposite end of the stage, winning a round of applause.

Li Sung did a few more minor feats of escapology, contortionism and acrobatics.

Murphy relaxed a little. This was more like it. A beautiful woman performing what he considered safe, normal trickery. It wasn't quite on Houdini's level but it sure beat the violent, anarchic slapstick of the previous performances. He was far more comfortable watching this.

That sense of comfort evaporated when a sinister-looking guillotine was trundled on stage by her accomplice.

If the previous acts were anything to go by Murphy had a bad feeling about how this was going to end. His suspicions were to prove right, for, after failing to escape from the locking mechanism which held her head in place, the blade sliced down — cutting through air, then silk, then flesh; decapitating Li Sung.

Accompanied by a splash of blood and much screaming from the audience, her severed head rolled to one side.

Down came the curtain.

Murphy rubbed his jaw. This Chung-Fu was one sick individual. Yes, it was all trickery; dummies and fake blood, and he bet that right now the various performers were backstage in their squalid dressing rooms, smoking cigarettes and removing their make-up, no doubt getting ready to hit the bars — but the man was still sick. This bloody production was testament to that. Looking around him he could see that less than a dozen others remained in the audience, those strong-stomached ones who had chosen to stay to the end. And a few who were probably too drunk to move.

The old man returned once more.

'And now, for the highlight of tonight's cabaret. With no further ado, may I introduce the master of Oriental magic,

Chung-Fu.' He threw down his knobbly walking stick and raised his hands. Holding his pose, he began to levitate.

Murphy stared, intrigued.

Then with a bang and a flash of smoke and a roll of drums from some hidden orchestra pit, the old man cast off his tattered robes. A bright, almost blinding light shot forth and when Murphy's sight cleared he saw that a mid-air transformation had taken place.

The old man was gone and another, much younger man, the man he had seen on the poster, Chung-Fu, was there. Dressed in a truly expensive silken robe of purple, gold, red and black, and wearing his tasselled cap he stared out, his eyes piercing. Tracing a mystic sign in the air before him, the magician conjured flames from his hands before descending to the stage. Strange Chinese words came from his mouth.

Shadowy snakes and tigers sprang into being behind the menacing figure, silhouetted against the curtain. And then it seemed as though the shadows detached themselves, spilling out to embrace the walls of the theatre, to encircle those within.

'What the hell?' muttered Murphy, staring around at the encroaching darkness. Over to one side he could see some other men getting ready to leave.

Fang-filled, monstrous shadow-shapes flowed and slithered. Like a voracious mould they seemed to spread and drip, flowing down walls and oozing across the stained, popcorn-littered carpet of the theatre. Some of the shadows seemed to fight each other, the larger, fiercer ones devouring the lesser ones.

None of this was real, Murphy tried to tell himself. A demoniacal miasma had fallen and icy fingers crept up his spine, ruffling the small hairs on the back of his neck. Terror surged through him as he continued to watch the spreading of the ghastly shadows. This was sheer nightmarish horror and he knew it.

'Well gentlemen,' spoke Chung-Fu. 'I see you've enjoyed tonight's cabaret. If you hadn't you wouldn't still be here.'

A thick-set man in the second row got up, fastening his raincoat.

'I'm afraid you'll find that you're unable to get out.' The conjuror smiled wickedly.

'What d'ya mean?' shouted the man.

Chung-Fu paced to the edge of the stage. 'I mean this is the end. For you all.' The sorcerer pointed and stared.

Whether it was due to some form of hypnotism, Murphy couldn't tell, but the man with the raincoat seemed to stop, become immobile.

'To some I am a devil. To others I am but Chung-Fu. Regardless, it is my place to prepare you for my next show. You've damned yourselves by staying and drinking in the bloodshed and the violence. You had the chance to leave, to follow your better judgement, but instead you chose to stay. And like those from my last performance *you* will become part of my new act.'

'Not bloody likely!' Another man got up and made a run for it. Others screamed and clamoured to get out. This was now a stampede; a mad exodus of theatregoers desperately trying to get out.

All hell broke loose.

Snapping shadows flowed from the walls and, horrifyingly, Murphy saw one unfortunate swallowed whole, disappearing into a tenebrous maw. Gun in hand, he made a dash for where he thought the exit lay, but in the poor light it was hard to be certain.

It was chaos. Screams and wails reverberated around the walls of the fleapit. Some were trampled in the side aisles. Another man was dragged, kicking and screaming, by a shadowy tentacle that pulled him against a wall. With unbelieving horror, Murphy saw the individual engulfed, absorbed by shadow. One moment he was there, the next, nothing but inky blackness!

Insanity threatened to take him. By some extreme mental effort, he managed to force it down, to focus on staying alive. He would willingly spend the rest of his days in the nuthouse if it meant getting out of this hell.

Then he and four others were at the doors. They were locked.

'*Move it!*' Murphy shouted, pushing aside one of the others and blasting two bullets at the lock. He then kicked the door open.

Brighter light struck them.

Then pandemonium spilled out into the foyer as several of the stagehands came charging at them. The first went down with a slug between the eyes. He fell and exploded — just like the goon who had attacked him in his apartment.

'Sweet Jesus!' shouted one man.

'Get out! Everybody out!' yelled Murphy, discharging another round, downing another explosive-filled attacker. He made a mad rush for the outer doors. Shadows and other horrors poured out after them, closing in.

Then the main theatre doors crashed open.

Three men armed with Thompson submachine guns stood in the doorway, framed against the light flung from the street lights outside.

'That you, Murphy?' one of them shouted. 'What the hell's going on?' It was 'Muscles'.

'Get outta here!' Turning, Murphy fired

a few more shots and ran to join them.

There followed a yammering of sub-machine gunfire as the hoodlums riddled the foyer with bullets. There were screams and shouts as dark things swelled and vanished, bubbled forth and retreated, ebbed and flooded. More of those strange, explosive-filled 'men' joined the carnage. The air was filled with the smell of gunpowder.

Murphy's mind darkened, unwilling or unable to take in any more of the unfolding madness. He was vaguely aware of a pair of strong arms dragging him clear of the theatre.

★　★　★

Maxwell wasn't buying any of it. He stood, his back to Murphy, gazing out the window onto the rain-washed street below.

'But it's true, boss,' said 'Muscles', 'there were some weird things going on. I saw it.'

'Listen to what your man's telling you,' added Murphy. 'That goddamned China-man's — '

Maxwell spun round to face them. '*What? The Devil?*' He strode over to his desk. 'And that somehow he's turned 'Two-Bellies' and Huey Labada into freakin' glove puppets? Come on, what kind of idiot would believe that?' He pointed directly at Murphy. 'Nobody makes an idiot outta me. *Nobody!* You got that?'

'Sure, I've got that.' Murphy nodded. He was still trying to come to terms with the horrors of the show he had seen the other evening. Now, in the relative sanity of Maxwell's office, with the grey light of morning shining in through the window, he tried to tell himself that some of it had been but stage trickery. *Some of it* — that was the problem. If only he could convince himself that *all* of it had been nothing more than elaborate theatricals effects.

'But what about the men that exploded, boss?' It was 'Muscles' who raised the question.

Maxwell shook his head. 'I don't know. That could be anything. Maybe they weren't real to begin with. Maybe you just thought they were real. Dummies or something.' It was clear he didn't have a good answer for this.

'And 'Two-Bellies'?' asked Murphy. 'Okay, maybe that thing I saw wasn't him but surely you agree it's highly coincidental that his name is being used? And Labada, I remember now. He was one of those that helped spring 'Two-Bellies' out of Bridewell, wasn't he?'

'So what are you saying?'

'I'm saying that maybe he and 'Two-Bellies' were pals. Maybe they went to one of these shows together. And, even if you don't think that spooky Chinaman has supernatural powers, I'd say it still suggests that something happened to them there, at one of his shows. It's just too coincidental for their names to be used and for one to appear as a mobster, the other a jailbird.'

'This is getting nuts. But maybe you're right.' Maxwell frowned. 'Well, let's not get the cops involved. That's the last thing we need right now.' He looked Murphy dead in the eye. 'What do you suggest? I mean, you've seen this man. You claim to know what he's capable of.'

'Well that's just it. I'm trying to forget just what he's capable of. Madness and magic, what more can I say? If the Devil does exist I'd say he's living somewhere in Chinatown, Chicago.'

'Right, I've had enough of this.' Maxwell reached into a drawer and withdrew an automatic. He looked to his henchman. 'Devil or not, he's made a big mistake in muscling in on my patch. Get the boys together. Tell 'em that we're going to sort out a little business in Chinatown. Tell 'em to come armed. And get Larry 'the lips' on the phone. He'll know where this slant lives.' He clicked home a magazine. 'It's time I paid this Chung-Fu a visit and put him straight about who runs this freakin' town.'

* * *

Four cars filled with hoodlums rendez-voused on one of the wide streets opposite the Dow-Tung Restaurant. A typical pork and noodles joint, it was frequented by all manner of unsavoury types: immigrants, railroad workers, dockhands and bums.

This was where Larry 'the lips' had said Chung-Fu held out.

'You ready for this, Murphy?' asked Maxwell, looking out of the car window at the sleazy establishment across the road.

'I don't know.' It was an honest enough answer. He had seen things the other night that had dragged his sanity to the verge of breaking point, stretched it like toffee. And who knew what fresh terrors awaited them now? Just how effective would bullets prove against the terrible magic of Chung-Fu?

'Let's do this.' Maxwell got out of the car.

More car doors opened and a dozen men in long coats, their weapons concealed beneath, stepped out and followed him.

Murphy walked along behind them.

Pushing aside an old Chinese man who was smoking something suspicious from a long clay pipe, Maxwell went up to the front door of the restaurant and kicked it open. He then fired a shot in the air. 'I'm looking for Chung-Fu,' he shouted.

There was immediate silence. Confused, wrinkled faces turned to look.

'I know some of you speak English, so I'll ask once more. Where's Chung-Fu?'

No one answered.

Maxwell shot a man nearby. 'I'll keep shooting till someone tells me.'

The crowd inside grew hostile but their hostility turned to fear when they saw Maxwell's heavies gathered in the doorway, their Tommy guns and double-barrelled shotguns out. Murphy peered from within their ranks.

Maxwell pointed his gun at another man. His heavy-handedness got results.

'I tell, I tell!' The man raised his arms.

'Where?'

'Chung-Fu, he leaving for China. He being taken to shipyard. He decide he live here no more. He take man with two bellies with him, some others and he go.'

'*Two bellies?*' Maxwell snarled. '*Two-Bellies?!*'

'Little man in crate.'

'Never mind a crate, I'll put him in a box six feet under if he's joined forces with the Chinaman.' Maxwell aimed the gun. 'Which dock?'

'I think he say six.'

'Are you going to go after him?' asked Murphy.

'You bet I'm going to go after him. I hate leaving loose ends. Nobody crosses Teddy Maxwell and gets away with it.' The mob boss returned his gun to its holster and turned to his men. 'Some of you remain here in case this son of a bitch is lying. You see Chung-Fu, you shoot him like the rat he is.' He looked at Murphy. 'Right. You and me are going to the dock. There's a shipment bound for China that ain't gonna get there.'

* * *

'Why do you think he's getting out?' asked Murphy as the car, driven by one of Maxwell's men, sped for the St. Lawrence docks. Evening was fast approaching and it was getting dark and foggy.

'Don't know. Don't care. Maybe your visit the other night got him rattled. Maybe he thinks he's going to get busted. I'll teach him. What say you, 'Muscles'?'

'You got it, boss,' came the laconic reply from the back seat.

'And what's this about 'Two-Bellies' being in a crate?' asked Murphy.

'Maybe he can't afford a second-class ticket.' Maxwell grinned.

Their surroundings became increasingly derelict and threatening. This was a foreboding, heavily built-up area that attracted some of the worst of human society. All manner of lawlessness took place here. Especially when, like now, the sun was going down.

Murphy felt uneasy. He had done so ever since Maxwell had declared his intentions of pursuing Chung-Fu. Inwardly, he couldn't help but think that it was the wrong decision, that nothing good would come of it, that it would only pile evil upon evil. Better to let him go and take his weirdness back to the Orient. He was now convinced that there was something unnatural about the other, some thing that went well beyond the normal and the understandable. What he had witnessed he could no longer, despite his best attempts, assign to the realm of trickery and illusion.

'Right, 'Weasel'. Look out for dock six,

should be getting near. I remember a few years back sending some loser to the bottom with concrete shoes on near here.' Maxwell laughed.

The driver slowed down. In the fog it was hard to make out anything. The dockyard was silent. The great hulks of berthed ships and container vessels formed murky shadows.

'Weasel' noted a sign. 'Dock six.' He turned the car around and drove slowly in the direction shown.

Before them loomed a massive Trans-Atlantic steamer. A few dockhands moved around, loading crates and boxes of provisions and necessities. Apart from that there was little other real activity.

'They're loading her up. Looks like she's getting ready to depart in the morning,' said 'Weasel'.

'Yeah. In which case we've got to get to Chung-Fu now. Pull over.' The car came to a stop. 'Right, leave the talking to me.' Maxwell got out.

Murphy, 'Weasel' and 'Muscles' got out.

Purposefully, the mob boss strode

towards one of the workmen. 'Any passengers boarded yet? A strange-looking Chinaman? Might have had a few others with him, including a big fat guy with a scar down the left side of his face.'

'There were a couple of Chinese guys came just over an hour ago. Queer-looking folk. Didn't say much. Told 'em they'd have to wait till the foreman got here in the morning afore we could load 'em aboard. They weren't too happy, so we sent 'em down to loading bay thirteen. Why are you asking? You a cop?'

'Yeah, I'm a cop,' Maxwell lied glibly. 'They're shipping opium and guns out of the country. We gotta confiscate that contraband. Bay thirteen, you say?'

'Yeah. Just along there a bit.'

'Thanks.'

Maxwell, Murphy, 'Weasel' and 'Muscles' headed off in the direction given. It was strangely eerie in the deserted, evening docks. Everything was shadowy, gloomy, filled with a haunting apprehension.

The loading bays were huge, warehouse-type structures.

A cold chill crept into Murphy; a damp

feeling that seemed to leak into his soul, filling him with fear. He found himself breathing heavily, mist forming before his face, fogging his vision further. There was evil here, of that he was certain; an evil that went far beyond Maxwell's thuggishness; an evil born of age-old wickedness, an evil that could be considered otherworldly. Unlike the others, with the possible exception of the dim-witted 'Muscles', he had experienced that evil. He knew just what it was capable of. And that knowledge made him starkly afraid, filled him with a soul-draining dread.

'Right.' Maxwell stood before the warehouse door. 'I want 'Two-Bellies' alive. I ain't too bothered about the others, although if you can take 'em alive, do so.' He gave the door a push.

The four of them crept inside.

It was dark and gloomy. Reaching for a light switch, Maxwell flicked it on.

The building was huge. It was filled with crates, boxes and all manner of containers, some bearing stencilled lettering regarding either their provenance or their destination, all lit up by rows of overhead light bulbs.

There was movement up ahead. Shadowy figures crouched behind some of the containers, clearly surprised at this intrusion.

'Spread out,' Maxwell ordered.

No sooner had his order been given than a gunshot shattered the silence, a bullet ricocheting off a nearby wall. They all immediately took cover, ducking behind crates. Two more shots rang out.

'Seems Chung-Fu's here and he means business,' said Maxwell, turning to Murphy. Gun in hand, he crept forward, taking cover behind a row of crates.

Stealthily, Murphy edged his way to one side. His nerves were tingling, although this was with a fear that he was able to cope with. He had been in numerous situations like this — bullets whizzing over his head and fighting thugs more than willing to end his life. This was normality, as far as he was concerned. Creeping forward, using crates for cover, his index finger clammy on the trigger of his .38 revolver, he moved almost silently, sneaking around the side, hoping to gain the advantage by getting behind the shooters.

There were two of them: Chinese in appearance, although Murphy would have bet a month's wages that they were more of those firework-stuffed mannequins he had encountered before. They were crouched low, their guns at the ready. He doubted whether he could take out both of them before they were to return fire. Then he saw 'Muscles' creeping from one side, his Tommy gun in his hands. He signalled for him to hold his ground. This would have to be handled carefully.

Ducking low, Murphy edged a little closer.

And then the Chinese men were shooting. Whether at Maxwell or 'Weasel', Murphy wasn't sure. They were standing, making good targets, and he knew now was the time to open fire. Aiming for a second, he squeezed the trigger, the recoil hammering at his wrist. Bullets flew.

One of the men went down, exploding against a chest-high heap of crates with a loud bang. 'Muscles' opened fire on the other, a storm of bullets blasting forth in a fiery burst, tearing the remaining man apart. He too exploded.

And then a crate over to one side sprang open and Chung-Fu burst on to the scene. Only this was not the virile, powerful Chinese sorcerer Murphy had last seen at the weird theatre but rather the ancient, wrinkled, cadaverous old man who had introduced the acts. In fact his appearance was many times worse than that. His skin was grey and corpse-like, almost mummified. His face was ghastly; red eyes glaring, crooked lips drawn back over protruding fangs. His hands were extended claws, the nails long and talon-like. There was a supernatural horror about him that filled all of them with fear.

'What the hell?' exclaimed Maxwell, rushing up and discharging a round of bullets at the hideous thing.

The bullets had no effect whatsoever.

'Muscles' opened fire, emptying a drum of submachine gun bullets. And then 'Weasel' was shooting. Crates were splintered and blown asunder. In the resulting chaos, Maxwell fell forward, blood trickling from the corner of his mouth. He had been shot three times in the back.

Murphy turned to look. Crawling forward, a smoking revolver in its hand, came 'Two-Bellies' — the deformed, dummy-imp in the convict costume. What manner of perverse sorcery Chung-Fu had used to transform the fat gangster into this foul abomination, he had no idea, nor had he any desire to stay around in order to find out. He pulled back, eyes staring as Chung-Fu rose into the air. A dark cloud began to form around him. His eyes became lambent, red fires of pure evil.

The terror-shadows began to grow, snuffing out the light.

This was an enemy Murphy knew could not be beaten. This was an ancient, demonic thing, no doubt an entity that had existed for centuries, its power derived from the horror it instilled in others; a vampire of sorts. He turned and ran for the exit. 'Weasel' was already there, his face chalk-white, his body trembling.

There came a scream as something terrible befell 'Muscles'.

The thing that had been Harry 'Two-Bellies' Lafayette fired, bullets whining past Murphy's head.

'There's some dynamite in the car,' shouted 'Weasel'. Together he and Murphy dashed outside into the natural dark of evening and ran to the parked vehicle. Several curious dockhands, alerted by the gunshots, watched from a safe distance.

Heart pounding fiercely, Murphy stood trying to gain his breath, waiting as 'Weasel' flung open the boot and removed several sticks of dynamite. He handed them to Murphy before taking out some more.

Murphy glanced back at the warehouse. Hideous, unnatural things were happening in there within its shadow-filled interior. For an instant, his vision blurred, veiled by the falling rain. He blinked his eyes clear. Then horror burst out anew as he saw the demonic thing that stood in the doorway of the warehouse, grinning at him with a leering smile. The features were indistinct, half-visible through the black, suffocating shadows that billowed out around it.

Then 'Weasel' was lighting fuses and throwing his sticks of dynamite.

An almighty explosion destroyed the doorway of the warehouse. A second and then a third blast went off, the powerful detonations throwing fire and wood skywards. A wall of fiery heat struck Murphy as he hesitated before hurling his explosives. The two men then pulled back, waiting, hoping that nothing would emerge from the conflagration that now raged before their eyes. Thankfully, nothing did.

They then got in the car and sped off, leaving behind the madness of Chung-Fu and the bodies of Maxwell and 'Muscles'.

* * *

Hang-Lee, the government-appointed investigator, examined the poster that had appeared overnight on the wall of the run-down cinema. There had been a rash of disappearances in the Poor Quarter of Beijing . . .

'Freddy'

If it was real, then surely it was something that should never have existed.

Colonel James Mortimer Stanthorpe was wheeled into the large reception room of his sprawling country mansion by his twenty-two-year-old grandson, David, in order to meet and greet the thirty or so invited guests. Wheelchair-bound, white-haired and in his mid-eighties, he still looked like a man who could handle himself in a tight spot. Like his father, who had served under Lord Kitchener, his had been a long, distinguished and highly decorated career. Some of those gathered were distant family members, military friends and colleagues he had spent time with out in India. Others were appropriate dignitaries, and there were also one or two from the local press.

Kyle Thorndyke was one of the latter, getting to rub shoulders with the great and the good of British society. He was in his early thirties, tall and lanky, with blue eyes and prematurely greying hair. Taking a glass of champagne from a tray carried by a passing waiter, he tried to blend in, become inconspicuous. It was something he was particularly skilled at: the ability to fade into the background when the need arose, and yet become noticed by those that mattered when he desired.

The champagne was excellent and, taking a sip, Thorndyke sauntered over to where the retired colonel was now holding court, a small group gathered around him.

'Can I just say how pleased I am to see you all here today. I never expected there to be quite so many. Maybe I didn't think that my father's collection would prove to be of such interest. We can begin the tour as soon as everyone's ready,' announced Stanthorpe in his plummy voice — a dyed-in-the-wool, authoritative, military voice. He talked in a way that commanded respect.

Chatting animatedly amongst themselves, the guests began to congregate near the large double doors that led from the room.

'I would like to say a few words before we go in.' Stanthorpe cleared his voice. 'The collection that you're about to see represents some forty years of my father's life, with curios and artefacts gathered from his many travels abroad. And whilst the majority of the collection originates from India, where both he and I were stationed for what seems like an eternity now that I look back on it, there are bits and pieces from all over the world. Some he bought from traders. Some he actually found in the long-lost temples scattered all over the Near and Far East. I could go on, but I think I've gone on long enough, as no doubt some of you would agree. So, please, let us go in. Feel free to take photographs. If you've any questions about any of the curios do ask. If I can't answer your question — then, I can't answer your question.'

This got some chuckles from the expectant crowd. Some, particularly the academics, were chomping at the bit to view the collection of the weird and the wonderful. Others were there solely for the champagne and the delicious canapés.

Thorndyke was there to take a general look and, if lucky, have a one-to-one with Stanthorpe, get some juicy material for the column he would write for his paper. Maybe get something with a bit of derring-do from the old man, something with a hint of adventure and mystery — things he could later embellish and romanticise to garner interest and boost readership. His editor had informed him that a dry account of whatever old relics the retired colonel might have assembled would not be good enough. It wouldn't sell. Consequently, he had to get something a bit meatier and, a bit like the stuffed tiger he was now passing, he liked to consider himself a bit of a predator, stalking down stories.

It was a museum of sorts that they entered; a repository of the mundane, the weird and the wonderful, lit solely by authentic, tallow-dripping, flaming torches, giving it a slightly menacing atmosphere. The main entrance was flanked by leering, fanged, tongue-protruding statues of

59

grotesque beings that stood sentinel by the doorway. Inside, there were numerous glass cabinets in which a wide range of mysterious items of exotica was on display: tribal dresses, jewellery, weapons and other odds and ends. One side room had been devoted purely to works of a religious nature, with several marble statues of various Hindu deities and lavish wall coverings. Incense burned in censers attached to the walls to provide a bit of extra ambience.

The guests spread out. Champagne glasses in hand, they strolled around. There was some banter, small talk, and a few photographs taken. Some remained chatting to Stanthorpe.

Thorndyke had to admit none of the material on display particularly interested him. Yes, some of the things were odd, such as the neatly ordered assemblage of tiny man-like statues that seemed almost too lifelike or the strange collection of carved, skull-painted death masks, which hung on one wall. There was even a huge, stuffed saltwater crocodile, suspended from wires, its jaws spread wide. It was a true monster, perhaps thirty feet or so in length. In the main, though, at least as far as he was concerned, it was just one man's amassed junk.

He spent another quarter of an hour or so walking around, pretending to look interested.

A sign on the stairs that led down indicated that there was more to the exhibition in the room below, so Thorndyke hastily went in that direction, hoping to be the first to get there. There was a door before him, which he opened, finding himself in a smaller room. Unlike upstairs, this room was lit by electric lights and, whereas above the spacing of the exhibits had been more open, down here it was much more constrained, the rows of cabinets separated by narrow walkways. It was the kind of place where one accidental trip could bring down everything.

With that thought in mind, Thorndyke gingerly stepped inside. To his untrained eye, the displays in here were much the same as those above. There were more collections of antiquated forms of weaponry as well as some pieces of strange,

Oriental-looking clothing. The shelves of one cabinet were strewn with hundreds of old coins. Below that were some ancient pieces of pottery.

Carefully walking between the display cabinets, Thorndyke panned his eyesight up and down, side-to-side, taking in the plethora of the weird and the unusual. In essence it was just more of the same; antiques and trophies, oddities and —

Thorndyke stopped. *What on earth was this?* He stooped low in order to better examine the stuffed thing — dare he call it an animal? — that stood upright in the glass cabinet before him. It was about the size of a large monkey, but there all real comparison ended. For a start, it had two heads, the larger one positioned atop the neck like that of most bipedal creatures, whilst the second protruded from high up on its right flank. Both heads were repulsive in appearance, bearing such ghastly features as two-inch-long fangs, bulging, unsightly eyes and bat-like ears. The nose on the larger head was flattened; that on the smaller, beak-like. The larger head also looked warped, half-melted, the left side reduced to a sagging flap of drooping flesh. Its torso was shallow-chested, its ribs clearly visible beneath the taut skin. Short, coarse brown hair covered most of it in mangy patches. A pair of half-formed, membranous wings lay flat against its knobbly-spined back. Both arms were extended, vicious clawed hands spread wide. Its legs were spindly, the three toes of one foot splayed like that of a chicken, the other more man-like. A sinuous tail sprouted from its rear end. There was something both reptilian and mammalian about it; an unnatural hybridisation. One could even go so far as to say an *incompleteness* — almost as though it had been killed mid-way through some kind of horrible transformation. For killed it had been — a slender bolt of brass sticking from its abdomen.

A tattered display sign, yellowed with age and written in bold letters, merely said: 'Freddy'.

Thorndyke was aware that he had been joined by a plump woman and her tall husband, an ex-military man if ever there was one — clean-shaven, dignified, his back ramrod straight. Two Indian men came down after them. They were looking about curiously and talking to one another in a language he didn't understand.

'I see you're admiring my great-grandfather's little pet.'

Thorndyke turned. He had not heard the other approach but he recognised David Stanthorpe. He turned his gaze back on the thing in the cabinet. 'What is it? And why call it 'Freddy'?'

'Your guess is as good as mine. Ugly little blighter though, isn't it?'

'I don't think I've ever seen anything like it in all my life. It's not like any animal I've ever seen or read about. Obviously it's a hoax. I mean, surely the two heads is a bit of a giveaway? It looks more like a kind of patchwork animal — monkey, rooster, vampire bat. A stitched-together monstrosity. A bit like what they did with that Piltdown man-thing, where some idiot stuck an orang-utan's jaw onto a human skull in order to try and baffle the experts.'

'My grandfather might know more

about it. What I can tell you is that it's been in the family a long time. I think it must have been my great-grandfather who found it and called it 'Freddy'. Used to give me nightmares as a boy.'

'I can see why.'

'Anyway, I'm afraid to have to inform you all that my grandfather's not feeling too well and that unfortunately he's decided to retire for the day.'

'Oh, nothing serious, I trust?' asked the tall man.

'No, I think it's just the sense of occasion that's finally got to him. He's eighty-three, you know. Doesn't look it and he certainly doesn't act it. I believe he's planning to reopen the exhibition next week some time when hopefully he's feeling better, so I do hope you can all make it. There's a full room of stuff upstairs that I've still to go through.' David smiled. 'I'm sorry about this but obviously I've got to consider my grandfather's health first and foremost.'

'But, can't we stay and have a look around?' asked the woman. 'We've come all the way from Oxford.'

'Come dear, let Colonel Stanthorpe have his rest. We can always come back next week. It's not as though these things are going anywhere, now is it?' replied her husband.

Thorndyke was annoyed. It looked like he wasn't going to get the chance to ask the old man about anything, at least not today. Resignedly, he followed David and the others back up the stairs. Well, that had been an almighty waste of time, he thought as he was guided out of the mansion.

★ ★ ★

That night, Thorndyke tossed and turned in the throes of a terrible nightmare. One moment everything was black and empty, a nebulous void, and then a speck appeared, growing larger. He tried to look away, to scream, for as the image became clearer he realised it was that horror in the cabinet, that unidentifiable creature, 'Freddy'. It was motionless, suspended almost in a whirling vortex and then, the thin brass bolt slipped from its side as though pulled by an invisible hand. Suddenly all four of its eyes opened, revealing vertical, violet pupils. Its arms jerked as though controlled by a diabolical puppeteer. It began jigging a crazy dance, leaping and hopping from one foot to the other. Dark red blood bubbled and slavered from its twin mouths.

And then there was a sound in Thorndyke's ears, in his mind. An unearthly, high-pitched piping that sawed through his brain; a truly fiendish noise. Voices accompanied the soul-burning music, male voices chanting, humming, crying. It rose in crescendo to a demoniacal cacophony, like the wailing of a thousand tortured souls crying out for an end to their suffering.

And then 'Freddy' came closer, filling his entire inner vision. The hideous eyes in those twin heads glared at him, fixing him with a malignancy not born of this earth. Its mouths opened and some form of foreign, alien speech that he had never heard spoken before poured out, shaping words that meant nothing to him. A clawed hand came up, reaching out for him, ready to grasp and tear, to scratch and rend, to pull him to pieces . . .

It was almost as if it was trying to get inside him, to become him.

* * *

It was his phone ringing just a few short hours later that finally woke him up. Throwing on a dressing gown, he rushed downstairs to answer it. It was still dark outside so he wondered who on earth it could be. He picked up the receiver.

'Thorndyke.' It was his editor; he recognised the voice immediately.

'Yeah, what is it?'

'I want you to get yourself over to the Stanthorpe place pronto. You were there yesterday, weren't you? Well, I've just had a tip-off from a friend in the police that something big's going on over there. I think there's been a break-in. Unconfirmed reports are that there has been at least one fatality.'

'Good God!'

'Get yourself over there and find out what's going on. If there's a story, I want you to be the first to it.'

'On my way.' Hastily, Thorndyke rushed upstairs and got dressed. Without stopping for any kind of breakfast, he threw on his jacket and left the house. He got in his car and sped towards the colonel's country mansion. Thankfully, there was hardly any traffic and twenty-five minutes later he pulled into the wide driveway, tyres crunching on the gravel of the large car park where an ambulance and three police cars were parked.

There were five policemen and a plain-clothes detective stood near the doorway.

Getting out of his car, Thorndyke grimaced somewhat as he saw two male ambulance staff emerge from the house carrying a stretcher, a white sheet covering the man-shaped lump underneath.

'Can I help you?' asked the plainclothes detective.

'My name's Thorndyke. I work for *The Gazette*.'

'Is that so? Well, clear off, can't you see we're conducting an investigation here? The last thing we need is someone from the press sticking their — '

Thorndyke saw David Stanthorpe come

out of the house. He looked withdrawn and shaken, but at least he was alive. Ignoring the policeman, he walked over.

David stared at him. It was abundantly clear he was suffering from shock. '*You?* What are you doing here?' he asked.

'What happened?'

The detective stepped between the two. He was facing Stanthorpe when he spoke. 'I'm sorry, sir. This man's from the press. I'll get rid of him if you want me to.'

'No, that won't be necessary. News of this will get out sooner or later. Perhaps the sooner the better. We have to find whoever did this and why.'

Thorndyke already had his notebook out. So far he had seen no sign of the colonel and he was now beginning to suspect the worst. After all, he had witnessed one body being taken out. Could be there were more in the ambulance. He would have to be tactful in his questioning. 'I understand completely if you don't want to tell me — ' he began.

'My grandfather was murdered in the early hours of this morning. Strangled. Killed in cold blood.'

'I am truly sorry. Please, accept my deepest condolences.' Thorndyke felt sorry for the other. What a tragic occurrence. 'If there's any way I can be of assistance I will.'

'There must be a connection between the opening of the exhibition and what happened.'

'Sir,' said the detective, 'we will obviously get round to an intensive search of the property to see if anything has been stolen, but in the meantime can I once more urge you not to tell this reporter anything regarding the details of your grandfather's death.'

'Why's that?' asked Thorndyke impudently.

David paused for a moment, clearly considering the detective's warning. He opened his mouth to say something, then closed it again, uncertain. It was clear he was contemplating just how much he could confide in this man whom admittedly he had only met yesterday. He had always considered himself to be a good judge of character, so in the end he spoke up, much to the policeman's displeasure: 'It's just that certain things were found near my grandfather's . . . body. Certain things to suggest that he was ritualistically murdered. Then there was also the positioning of his body. You see, I found him this morning lying dead in his museum, sprawled out before one of those infernal statues.'

'The goddess Kali, to be exact,' said the detective. 'The Hindu Death Mother. The Queen of the Night.' When the other two looked at him in surprise, he went on: 'I haven't been a policeman all my life. I studied anthropology and theology at Cambridge before joining the force.' He offered his hand to Thorndyke. 'Well, now that Mr. Stanthorpe has filled you in, I might as well introduce myself. Detective Inspector Carson, Jim Carson. I think I know who or rather what's behind Colonel Stanthorpe's murder. The method, the crushed larynx, no traces of blood, the positioning of the body — all the signs suggest to me a Thuggee assassination.'

'A what?' enquired Thorndyke.

'Thuggee? I've heard of them,' said David. 'It's a religious organisation or something, isn't it? An Indian sect?'

'Yes and no,' said Carson. He reached into an inner jacket pocket and removed a packet of cigarettes. Opening it, he offered one to the others but both declined with shakes of their heads. He then lit up and took a deep drag before exhaling a cloud of eye-watering cigarette smoke. 'Thuggee was a religion based on homicide, ritual murder and robbery all carried out in the name of Kali. Although long thought to have been wiped out by the British in the mid-nineteenth century, it's unlikely that it was completely eradicated. The Thugs' — the practitioners of Thuggee — favourite weapon was the garrotte with which they would sneak up on their victim and strangle them, a stealthy and silent means of murder. Sometimes they improvised, using a scarf, a knot tied in the middle to add extra pressure and crush the larynx. Their religious taboos prohibited them from spilling blood.'

'But even assuming this perverse cult is still active today in Britain, why target an old man in a wheelchair? Why go after Colonel Stanthorpe?' asked Thorndyke. His journalistic mind was working overtime, convinced that there was a juicy story here.

'Perhaps I could answer that question.' David had regained some of his composure and the shocked, vacant look in his eyes had faded. 'My grandfather and my great-grandfather were actively involved in stamping out this Thuggee cult, ensuring that it was no longer a threat. It seems that they weren't entirely successful.'

'You're going to have to make sure that no one enters the main museum until we've conducted a full forensic examination,' said Carson, addressing David.

'Of course. I'll also — '

'Freddy!' Thorndyke spluttered.

'What about Freddy?' David looked confused.

'I had a nightmare. That thing was in it.'

'Who the hell's Freddy?' enquired the detective, looking at David.

'Freddy's not a person. It's a . . . a specimen, an exhibit; one of those rare, inexplicable finds that my great-grandfather brought back from India. A stuffed monkey-thing.'

A terrible, irrational thought began to develop in Thorndyke's mind. For some uncanny reason he — no doubt as a result of his nightmare — had this strange feeling that the horror in the display cabinet was in some way linked to Colonel Stanthorpe's murder. In what way, he didn't know; after all it was nothing more than a long-dead, deformed monkey, tinkered about with by some warped taxidermist. And yet there remained that little kernel of nagging suspicion.

'I see,' said Carson. 'Well — '

'Have you checked to see if it's still there?' Thorndyke asked David.

'Come now. Surely if robbery had been the main incentive a thief would have gone for something far more valuable?' David replied. 'I mean, there are genuine treasures contained in the museum. Some of the items of jewellery are worth hundreds if not thousands of pounds. And they would be far easier to carry. I can't see anyone wanting to steal that tatty old piece of junk. Except perhaps one of those experts who try to prove the existence of strange creatures, such as the Yeti.'

'A cryptozoologist,' commented Carson.

'Yes,' David nodded.

'Can we just check?'

'I don't see what harm it'll do. We can skirt the main museum and go in through the stairs at the back. Follow me.' David led the way to the house and into the ground floor museum, the smaller one with the densely-gathered glass cabinets.

It came as little surprise to Thorndyke when they found that the glass cabinet in question had been smashed to pieces, reduced to a mass of scattered shards, its ghastly occupant missing.

'What's this?' queried Carson, bending down to pick up the slender brass spike that lay amidst the glass. It was the thing that had been pierced into the hideous, two-headed abomination that had been named 'Freddy'.

★　★　★

It was some two weeks later that Thorndyke got the telephone call from David Stanthorpe asking him to meet him at the house. He had only seen him once during that time — when he had attended the colonel's funeral — and had largely and intentionally kept a low profile, permitting the bereaved time to grieve and become accustomed to his solitude in the mansion.

Thorndyke had done some research of his own; finding out that both of the younger Stanthorpe's parents had been killed in an air crash and that he had no siblings. Hence, his devotion to his crippled grandfather. And now even he was gone, brutally slain by a member of a dark fraternity long-thought defunct — or so Detective Inspector Carson believed.

Upon arrival at the house, Thorndyke was warmly greeted by David, who welcomed him inside, guiding him into the study where a roaring fire blazed in the wide hearth.

'Would you care for a drink? Wine? Whisky?'

'Whisky.' Thorndyke sat back in his seat, looking about him at the crammed bookshelves and the various stuffed animal heads: tiger, moose, gorilla and sundry other creatures of which he was unsure. One looked like the head of a zebra but it could have been that of an okapi or something similar. At least these looked like real creatures, however, the kind of things one could see in a zoo, unlike 'Freddy'.

David returned, a glass of whisky in hand. 'There.' He sat down and reached for a rather tattered leather book that lay on the table before him.

'How have you been?' Thorndyke asked.

'Not too bad. I do miss my grandfather not being around, but I guess I've got no option but to persevere. It's what he would've wanted. Stiff upper lip, and all that.'

'I hope you don't mind me asking, but have there been any developments in the police investigation? I told them all that I could remember about the day of the exhibition. I'm sorry I was unable to give better descriptions of the other people I saw down in the room that day.'

'Carson's been able to interview Lord and Lady Morris, the couple who were there, but they've been unable to trace those two Indian men.'

'Do you think they may have some-thing to do with this?' Thorndyke took a sip from his glass. It was strong stuff.

'It's possible. Carson took details but alas he's been unable to make much progress. To tell you the truth, I think he and his team are floundering in the dark. I've no doubt he's a very intelligent man, but I think he's a bit out of his depth here. It's my belief, call it a theory if you like, that those men came specifically for 'Freddy' and that my grandfather heard their break-in and came downstairs to investigate. Anyway, the reason I asked you to come out here is because of what I found in this.' David opened the book he held to a marked page. 'It's written by my great-grandfather and some of it doesn't make for easy listening.'

Thorndyke sat back as the other began reading a strange and enthralling handwritten account about the time when his distant relative had been in India serving in the British Army. He told of his ancestor's missions to eradicate the Thuggee operatives and of how he and his men tracked one such gang back to their hidden temple stronghold in the Samdari Valley. The Thugs had been terrorising the inhabitants of a local village, murdering the villagers in the night and causing no end of mischief, assuming different guises, appearing to be friendly merchants, honest travellers and the like before revealing their true, murderous nature. Apparently this had been the standard Thuggee practice. Anyhow, once Colonel Henry Stanthorpe and his men entered the ancient temple there was carnage as they opened fire and gunned down many of the cultists. The surviving members of the Dark Brotherhood of merciless killers withdrew from this onslaught, retreating deeper into the bowels of the temple.

'Fascinating stuff, but — '

'Wait, it gets better,' David continued, reading from the battered book. He related how his great-grandfather's men fought their way out of a Thug ambush before they came to a truly horrendous place filled with dead and imprisoned villagers. They had then entered an inner sanctum wherein the most diabolical and murderous rites were performed before a large graven image of their infernal four-armed goddess, Kali. It was in this hellish chamber, filled with stomach-wrenching horror and the stench of the dead and the dying, that the brave colonel was to come face-to-face with dozens of Thuggee cultists. Much blood was spilled. Fighting their way through, shooting many dead, they targeted the leader. With a desperate cry to the Death Mother, knowing he was doomed, the high priest of the Thuggee cult threw down a curse on the British defilers, sacrificing himself by plunging a knife deep into his own heart.

'Good Lord!' Thorndyke was intrigued but unsure as to where any of this fitted in with tracking down the old man's murderer or murderers.

The remainder of the account told how Colonel Stanthorpe gave the order not to take prisoners, such was the barbarity of the crimes levelled at the Thuggee members. All were executed; not that many surrendered, preferring to die in the name of their cruel, bloodthirsty deity. Later that evening, after the army man had returned to his garrison headquarters, he was beset by evil visions and he came down with a terrible fever. The doctor could do nothing and it was as a last resort that he sought out the grateful village elder and shaman who informed him that he was cursed.

'This is where it gets weird, and although I've no reason to dispute anything that my great-grandfather records it gets, well, judge for yourself.' David went on, telling of how Colonel Stanthorpe became feverish, delirious, unable to discern reality, his own words telling of his sorry state clearly written at a date not contemporaneous with his suffering. He became filled with the terrible desire to eat human flesh. The village elder said that an evil spirit, a demon, a rakshasa, had stolen his soul and that the only way he could regain it was by killing the demon. And so, arming the colonel with a crossbow and a brass bolt inscribed with tiny sigils, the elder performed a ritual, exorcising the demon, drawing it out of its host. The description of that event and what happened next was perhaps intentionally vague; in addition many of the pages were missing, half-burnt and yellowed with age, making further reading difficult. It appeared however that the demon had been expelled from Colonel Stanthorpe, whereupon he had shot it even as it had turned to flee.

'*Freddy?!*'

'Freddy.' David nodded. 'As trophies go, I'd say that's got to be the ultimate. A demon. I've done some research on these things, these rakshasas. They were malign entities that lived on human flesh. They were shape-changers and magicians, masters of lies, trickery, deceit and illusion. Their favourite tactic was to assume the appearance of someone known to their chosen victim; a friend or accomplice. Then, when they'd gained their trust, they'd strike at the most opportune moment.'

'That can't be right. Surely, that's not what that thing is. It can't be. It doesn't make sense.'

'None of this makes sense.'

'Yes, but come on — *a demon*?'

'Well, whatever it is, someone was prepared to kill in order to get it.' David opened a drawer in the desk and removed the thin brass bolt. 'Could be that they thought they could restore it to life by removing this. In which case, if they have brought it back, this is the only weapon that will destroy it once more. I've already bought a crossbow that I got specifically made in order to shoot it. I've been practising, improving my accuracy, should the need ever arise.'

Thorndyke looked at the other, incredulity all over his face. 'You don't believe this, do you?'

'I no longer know what to believe. Perhaps my great-grandfather was merely delirious and dreamt up the whole thing. However, if this account is true, then it could be that there's an evil cult out there, an evil cult that is now in possession of a demon.'

* * *

It was the trail of murder and the spate of disappearances that finally led the police to the massive abandoned RAF hangars deep within the Surrey countryside some thirty miles from David Stanthorpe's mansion. Having got the tip-off from his editor that something significant was going down, something that might be related to the murder of Colonel James Mortimer Stanthorpe, Thorndyke had swung round to pick up David before making his way there.

The reporter had never been to this part of England before and the details he had been given had been vague at best. Luck was obviously smiling on the pair of them however, for they quickly found the place, the immediate wooded surroundings cordoned off and manned by policemen, some of whom were armed.

Detective Inspector Carson noticed them immediately. He strode over. 'Well, I wasn't expecting you two. The situation's a bit delicate. Seems that there are some thirty people in there. All foreigners.'

'*Thugs?*' asked David.

'I think so, but don't let on to any of the others. Far as they're concerned it's just a mad gathering of illegal immigrants who've decided to hole themselves up in some of these old hangars. Last thing anyone else needs to know right know is that we may be dealing with a suicidal cult of death-worshippers. Wouldn't exactly boost morale, if you get what I'm saying.'

'Of course,' Thorndyke agreed. 'We understand.'

'We've been carrying out surveillance

on them for a day or two now. We were fortunate to track them down, for they're sneaky customers who know how to cover their tracks. We think they may have been responsible for over twenty, maybe as many as thirty killings, in the surrounding area.'

'So what's your plan?' asked David.

'Well they know we're here so they're just lying low for the moment. We're doing the same. As you can no doubt imagine it's a tricky situation. One that could blow up into something really nasty. We've got an interpreter at hand. As soon as I give the order we'll march on in there and apprehend the whole bloody lot. If they don't come quietly then they'll be sorry.'

Knowingly, Carson patted his inside coat pocket.

'David thinks they may have a — ' Thorndyke had forgotten the name so he looked to his companion.

'A rakshasa,' finished David. 'I think they're possibly harbouring a rakshasa. I think that's what Freddy was.'

'*A rakshasa?* Now let me think.' Carson

mused this one over as he lit a cigarette and placed it between his lips. He had prepared himself for a hundred possible scenarios but not this. It was ludicrous, bordering on the insane. 'You're talking about a monster out of myth and folklore, right? What the hell gave you that idea? I know these Thuggee fanatics are real, but they're just deluded crazies. The idea that there's some kind of monster behind this is utter stupidity!'

'Maybe it is. Maybe it isn't. Whatever the case, I've come prepared for it,' David replied.

'I want you two to stay well out of this. You hear me? This is police work, first and foremost. If things turn nasty then leave it up to me and my men. We've got these beggars surrounded and the last thing I need is for you two to mess things up thinking you're going in there. You stay well back, behind the line. At all times!'

'That's alright by me, Inspector.' Thorndyke smiled. The last thing he wanted was to play the hero and go in there and take on a small army of homicidal maniacs unarmed. More so if David was right and they had something demoniacal with them, although this was something he couldn't bring himself to believe. Yes, there were no doubt some very dangerous and wicked men holed-up in there but the rational, logical part of his brain clung to the belief that that was all. Hell, that was enough, wasn't it? Why complicate and exacerbate what was already a highly volatile situation by bringing in the unholy and the supernatural?

A young Indian-looking man walked over, a loud-hailer in one hand. 'Should I try again?'

Carson nodded and blew cigarette smoke from his nostrils. 'Once more. Tell them to surrender and come out with their hands up. Failure to comply will result in a siege. Tell them we're all armed and that we have the necessary authorisation to shoot to kill. Tell them that resistance is futile and that they have nowhere to go.'

The interpreter headed off. Words were shouted in an Indian dialect, words that made no sense whatsoever to Thorndyke.

Twenty minutes passed and there had been no reply.

Several armed policemen milled around

expectantly. Thorndyke saw another police-man concealed in the bushes, staring through a pair of binoculars at the large, grey, warehouse-type building some three hundred yards away.

Carson checked his watch. He knew that this siege could not go on indefinitely and that sooner, rather than later, he was going to receive the orders from his superiors to launch an attack. This was unlike anything he had ever experienced before, yet he felt a tremor of exhilaration course through him at the prospect of leading his men into battle — for that's what it would undoubtedly be like, similar in many ways to frontline warfare with the notable difference that he hoped that these cultists weren't armed with guns. It was a chance he had to take. For if they were, then this had the potential of turning into a true bloodbath.

And so commenced the waiting game.

* * *

'Do you think it's wise waiting this long?' asked David. 'It's already getting dark. In another half hour or so it'll be completely dark.'

'I think that's when Carson plans to launch his raid on the hangars.'

Thorndyke was getting uncomfortable, having sat in the car for several hours, his back muscles cramping somewhat. But he was feeling more than physically uncomfortable. His mind was a turmoil of dark thoughts, cogitating unwelcomingly over a multitude of unpleasant scenarios. And then there was the 'Freddy' thing again. Just what the hell was that? And was it, as David certainly believed, even now lurking nearby? He dreaded the prospect of seeing that thing animate, sentient. It was only the thought of the scoop he might achieve by covering this story that kept him from leaving.

'I can't help but think that waiting till dusk is a bad idea. But I suppose he knows best. This is the kind of thing he trains for, wouldn't you think?'

'Personally, I don't think they rehearse for this kind of thing at Hendon. But you never know.' Thorndyke was about to step outside, to stretch his legs, when he heard a gunshot. He almost jumped out of his skin. 'What the hell?'

'Who's firing?' asked David, nervously.

Two more shots rang out.

Now that his initial surprise had gone, Thorndyke felt certain that the loud bangs had come from the other side of the hangars. Was the siege underway? Then there were shouts and cries from the policemen to his front and sides, and more gunshots in the distance. Far off he heard police dogs barking. He walked forward a few yards.

And then, without warning, a shadow loomed up behind him and fastened a garrotte around his neck, pulling it tight, cutting off his air supply, crushing his larynx. Frantic, he struggled, fingers clawing at his own throat. It was no good. The cord bit deeper and his eyes were streaming. He was forced to his knees. This was the end, his mind screamed at him. He was going to be asphyxiated. His world darkened.

And then David was there, grappling the would-be assassin, pummelling him to the ground, making him release his stranglehold on Thorndyke. All three of them collapsed. Shouting for help, David smacked in several hard punches.

Gasping for breath, Thorndyke crawled away from the melee. Through pain-wracked eyes, he saw Carson rush over, gun in hand. There was a single shot, and then David clambered to his feet.

'These devils are on the attack!' Carson shouted. 'They've obviously crept out under the cover of darkness and now they're on the offensive. If I were you I'd get in your car and get the hell away from this place. There's no telling where they'll pop up next. I've called for reinforcements but God knows when they'll get here.'

More sporadic gunshots rang out.

Voices called out in the twilight.

And then Carson was firing at a shadow that had sneaked around the side of the car. With a cry, the 'shadow' slumped to the ground.

Thorndyke rubbed his badly-bruised neck. He looked like someone who had just survived a hanging. Tears streamed from his eyes.

'I'm telling you to get out of here. Get

in your car and go. *Now!* While there's still time.' Carson peered all around, ready and more than willing, to shoot at anything hostile than might emerge from the gathering darkness. He had to restrain his impulse when one of his officers came over at a sprint, his face flushed with fear and exertion.

'Sir, we've lost some good men over on the far side. That said, we've regrouped over by the copse of trees and are awaiting your commands.'

'Right. It's time to go in. We'll give these murdering dogs what for. Make sure every man carries his torch and that their guns are at the ready. Tell them to shoot to kill. We can't — '

'Where's David?' Thorndyke asked, his voice tinged with concern.

'What?' Carson turned.

Thorndyke rushed over to the car and looked inside before turning to the detective. 'He's gone. He's taken his crossbow. That can only mean that he's gone after that thing he was on about. I think he's headed for the hangar.'

'The bloody fool!' Carson cursed

savagely. 'That's all we need. Alright, we've got to go after him.' He looked at the reporter. 'Change of plan. Maybe you'd better come with us in case we need to talk any sense into him. I figure he'll trust you more than he will me. Come on!'

Thorndyke wasn't ready for this one bit, but he didn't know what the alternative, short of abandoning the young deluded man, was. Without their intervention, their combined strength, David would certainly be killed — his sole reward for his recklessness and his rashness would be an early death, followed perhaps by being offered as a sacrifice, as had his grandfather, to a demonic goddess.

Crouching low, using whatever cover there was, Thorndyke went in pursuit of Carson and the police officer, heading for the closest hangar. From every direction came the sound of gunshots, cries and screams. There was no denying it — the place was now a battlefield, the death toll on each side slowly mounting. For what the Thuggee devotees lacked in firepower they made up for in stealth and

94

subterfuge, cunning and tenacity of spirit; their creed, their very ideology, based on the tenet, the belief, that killing was their sacred duty, their divinely allocated task. For them, murder was a way of life; a laudable pursuit.

Still, faith was to prove useless against a .38 special round bullet or a hefty thwack on the skull from a police truncheon, and the cultists soon found themselves on the losing side. More so when the vans filled with police in full riot gear appeared on the scene.

Thorndyke overheard some of Carson's conversation over his police radio, informing him that the situation was now, thankfully, by and large under control.

All that remained was finding David.

Carson edged to the perimeter of the huge hangar. From behind cover, he glanced inside before signalling the others over. 'Do you still think he's here?'

'I don't know,' answered Thorndyke. 'But surely we'd have seen him if he'd doubled back?'

They all sneaked inside, ready for anything, or so they thought. The hangar had been transformed from a huge area for housing aircraft into a ghoulish temple dedicated to Kali. To that end, the Thugs had erected a large, rather crude-looking and terrible idol of their four-armed deity. *Around the statue's neck had been draped a necklace of severed human heads!* There was worse to come: dead, decaying bodies secured to the walls, dismembered limbs and heads in urns, rotting corpses heaped in one corner. The stench was unbearable.

'Heavens above,' muttered Thorndyke, gulping at the monstrous, gruesome sights before his eyes.

There was nobody here though. Nobody living at least. They were just about to head out, thankful to be leaving this blood-drenched slaughter house when, to their relief, David staggered into the vast doorway, his crossbow in hand. He looked tired and weary. Blood smeared the left side of his face.

'I — I got it,' he stammered, crumpling to his knees.

Thorndyke and Carson rushed over, helping the young man up.

'Steady, man. Steady,' said Carson, helping David to his feet. Supporting him, he and the reporter carried him back to the car where many policemen were milling around, some nursing their own injuries.

Three ambulances were waiting on standby and after leaving David in the capable hands of the crew from one, Thorndyke went and sat in his car. He would have nightmares for many days, if not weeks, possibly months to come after what he had seen. The sights in that hangar, that modified temple, had been horrendous and no matter how he tried he just couldn't blot them from memory. Somehow, he managed to switch his thoughts to David, wondering just what he had seen. To even contemplate that that horror had assumed some semblance of life — He shuddered and then jumped when there came a tap on the car window.

It was David.

'The docs say I'm okay to go home. They say I've probably pulled some muscles in my right leg and this scratch down my face shouldn't be anything permanent.'

'Glad to hear it.'

'Right now I just want to get home. Rest and try and forget all I've seen.'

'Well, I too have seen enough. I'm going to have to write a piece for my paper regarding this. Though I doubt whether anyone'll believe a word of it.' Thorndyke started up the car engine as David got in and sat in the back seat. Had he been paying closer attention he might have noticed the evil grin and the violet glint in his passenger's eyes. *For the thing in the back seat wasn't David — it was 'Freddy'!*

Hour of the Witch

It was a question of which of them, if any, would still be there by daybreak.

John McQueen sat at his desk, idly going through the mail that had gathered over the last few days. He had been away from work suffering from a heavy cold, but now that he was back and feeling much better he thought it was high time that he started to make some money. For the past twelve years he had hired out his services as a private investigator, and although he had never had any significant cases his profession had earned him a steady income.

Most of his mail was humdrum: enquiries regarding whether or not he was available to assist in locating missing dogs, discovering the whereabouts of stolen property and even one letter from a suspicious wife seeking help in tracking down an errant and undoubtedly unfaithful husband. He was just about to consult his logbook of old unresolved cases when the office door opened and Mark Forsyth, his assistant, entered with a dark-haired woman, slim and pale with dark eyes and an oval-shaped face. She looked to be in her mid-forties.

'Mrs. Eleanor Campbell,' announced Forsyth, ushering the woman inside.

Somewhat surprised, McQueen got to his feet. 'Good morning. Please, take a seat.' He could see that the woman was nervous, her eyes never still, taking everything in.

'Mrs. Campbell has got quite an interesting proposition.' Forsyth drew up a chair, sat down and took a notebook and pen from his pocket.

'Well, Mrs. Campbell,' said McQueen, 'if you'll tell me what your problem is I'll see whether or not I can help.' Once she had sat down, he too took his seat.

'Just over a year ago my husband, Cameron, disappeared.' Mrs. Campbell removed a handkerchief from a pocket and dabbed at her eyes before returning it. 'He was an investigator like yourself, with the exception being that he delved into the supernatural. A paranormal investigator is what he liked to be known as.'

'*Professor Cameron Campbell?*' inquired McQueen, trying to remember some of the details of the disappearance of the renowned parapsychologist that had made the headlines. 'I recall reading something about that in the newspapers. Didn't something happen to him on one of his investigations?'

'Not just Cameron, but his entire team of researchers from Glasgow University. Five of them in total.' Mrs. Campbell shook her head, clearly trying to come to terms with just whatever it was that had happened. 'They'd carried out investigations at alleged haunted sites all over Britain, hoping to discover evidence to prove the existence of the supernatural. Cameron had been the team leader, an expert in the field of parapsychology, the one who did all of the research in tracking down places of psychic interest. If only he hadn't found out about that awful house on Jura.'

More details of the case were slowly

filtering back into McQueen's mind. 'Yes, I'm remembering more about it now,' he said. 'It was quite big news. All of them just disappeared, didn't they? The police carried out an intensive investigation both of the house and the surrounding area but no one was ever found. Without doubt, a very mysterious case.' He gulped as a little shiver of uncertainty went through him. 'You've obviously come to me to ask whether or not I'd be willing to carry out my own investigations regarding their disappearance, yes?'

She nodded. 'I was informed that you had some experience in such cases.'

'Not recently,' said McQueen. 'In fact, these days I'm something of a sceptic when it comes to the supernatural. I guess you could say I've seen too much but experienced too little. However, I must say I am rather intrigued by this and have been ever since reading about it. Clearly something happened out there at that godforsaken place, something that resulted in the disappearance of five people. Just what, well clearly there was something that the police were unable to discover.' He scratched at the day's growth of stubble on his chin.

'So you will help me? You'll take the case?'

McQueen took out a packet of cigarettes from a drawer, lit one and took a drag. 'What do you say, Forsyth?' he asked, looking at his assistant. 'Sounds interesting, doesn't it?'

'Certainly does,' replied Forsyth. 'Although I don't really see what new light we'll be able to shed on this. I guess the first thing we should do is head out to this house and see if there's any evidence to be found, anything which the initial investigation may have overlooked. If we turn up nothing, then perhaps we might get some valuable insights into the minds of those who vanished by tracking down any friends and relatives.'

'Maybe a look at the initial police report might help as well,' added McQueen.

'Yes,' agreed Forsyth. 'Although you know as well as I that ever since that new chief inspector took over getting our hands on such documentation has proved increasingly difficult.'

McQueen nodded in agreement. 'Yes, that may prove tricky.' He stubbed out the remains of his cigarette in an ashtray. 'But first, I'd like to ask you a few questions about your husband, if I may, Mrs. Campbell. I guess the most important question is, do you yourself have any notion regarding just what may have happened to him and his team?'

'I'm afraid not. I'm as baffled as everyone else. There was absolutely no reason for Cameron to go missing. And as for the others, well I've been in correspondence with some of the relatives and they're just as confused as I am. The last year has been sheer torture for me, not knowing what's happened. Sometimes I can cope with it, but — ' She broke down into a sobbing fit, reaching for her handkerchief once more. After a few moments, she looked up, her eyes tearful. 'Please, I need your help in this. I've come to expect the worst but it's the not knowing — that's what's really painful.'

McQueen and Forsyth exchanged concerned, yet uncertain glances. Was it something they could handle? McQueen seemed to think so, although he doubted whether their investigations would reveal anything of merit.

'I'm imploring you,' pleaded Mrs. Campbell. 'Please help me find my husband. I don't know who else to turn to. The police are no longer interested. I'll pay you whether you find anything or not. I'm certain there will be something that the police have overlooked. Some small clue which may reveal what happened to them out there.'

'Very well, Mrs. Campbell,' said McQueen. 'I will take this case on, although I can't make any promises regarding the outcome. I'll also add that it is a little outside my usual field of experience, however I will give it my full, undivided attention. Now, how soon do you want me to start?'

'As soon as possible. The sooner the better.' A bright intensity shone in Mrs. Campbell's pale face now that she had told her tale and had secured the private investigator's service. It was almost as if she was a different woman from the one who had entered the office a few minutes earlier. 'I plan to travel to Jura myself within the week. I trust that's not too much short notice for you?'

It was certainly short notice but McQueen had the suspicion that this case could well be a significant one. If he were to discover the true explanation behind the disappearance of Cameron Campbell then he would be made for life. An opportunity like this did not come knocking every day, that was for certain. 'Very well, I'll see to it,' he said, reaching for another cigarette. He lit up and inhaled the smoke, drawing it deep into his lungs. 'In the meantime, I'll see what I can find out about this house. What was the name of it again?'

'It has no name. Only a reputation. You see I've done my own research, and from what I can gather it's not really even a house. More of a ruin. A crofter's cottage, which has now been reduced to little more than four walls and a shattered roof.' Mrs. Campbell reached into a coat pocket and removed a small photograph that she handed over. 'As you can see, there's not much of it still standing. It was once the property of a Mr. Tam

McSweeney and his wife, Aggie. My husband's reasoning for it being haunted was based on some research he'd done which had suggested that the previous owner, an old crofter, had been killed by his wife sometime during the last century. She was reputed to have been a practitioner of the Black Arts, a witch.'

Looking at the photograph, nothing immediately suggested itself to McQueen. It was, after all, little more than a tumbledown farmhouse. The white walls were barely standing and the roof was sagging; just a jumble of criss-crossing timbers in places. Two small square windows and a dark doorway completed the unimposing structure. And yet, the more he looked at it, the more a strange sense of unease filtered into his mind. For a long time, he sat there, unable to think clearly, unable to wrench his eyes away. Whether due to some strange quirk of the lighting, shadows seemed to crouch around the deserted building where shadows ought not to be, and he felt mild nausea arising from the pit of his stomach as he continued to stare at the image.

This he immediately put down to an association of facts; nothing more than an acknowledgement that something inexplicable had happened to five people there. It was this alone, he reasoned, that caused his unease.

'Not much to look at, is it?' said Mrs. Campbell.

'No, I guess not.' McQueen handed the photograph to Forsyth, who looked at it with measured interest. 'So, Mrs. Campbell, I've told you that I am willing to take on this case. It will necessitate quite some organisation but I'm pretty confident about being able to join you at the weekend. Just to let you know, I always work with my assistant, in fact some would say he's the brains of the outfit.'

'And you're the brawn?'

McQueen smiled. 'Hardly. So don't go expecting any gumshoe-like behaviour from me. I don't drink cheap whisky, and as you can see I don't operate from a sleazy backstreet office, nor do I carry a gun. Unfortunately the law in this country forbids me from using one — not that I foresee the need for one, for if I see anything ghost-like I'll be first out of the door.'

* * *

Four days later on the ferry crossing from the mainland to Port Askaig on Islay, McQueen stood next to Forsyth looking out across the churning grey water as the Paps of Jura, the name given for the three island mountains, loomed before them. It was cold, slightly foggy and very damp. And for those who had lived all of their lives as city-dwellers it was an imposing, foreboding and not particularly welcoming sight. It was no longer hard to imagine that something utterly inexplicable could have happened out here. It seemed as though they were going back in time; back to a remote past long-shrouded in myth and legend.

Having talked with the few passengers on board, most of whom were inhabitants of Islay, the closest island, they discovered that there were probably fewer than fifty islanders on Jura and that they would have to cross on the Feolin Ferry to reach their destination, where it was planned they would rendezvous with Mrs. Campbell.

'Quite an impressive sight, wouldn't you agree?' commented McQueen. 'Though just why anyone in their right mind would want to live out here beats me.'

'I daresay you get used to it after a while. The solitude, the cold, the rain. In summer, one of the men downstairs was telling me, the midges here are diabolical. They're like mosquitoes. The sooner we're away from here the better. I don't like it one bit.'

'Well, although we didn't manage to get a look at the police report, if we can find something of significance regarding the disappearance of Cameron Campbell and his team we'll be famous. Think of that while you're having to put up with the hardships. Besides, I think our investigations will only take a day or two at most. We've got sufficient camping gear to stay in that place in reasonable comfort and then we'll be back in Glasgow. And like Mrs. Campbell said, we get paid whether or not we find anything. So it's a win-win situation for us.'

'I don't suppose you've ever considered the possibility that there just may be something behind all of this? You know, something *weird*.'

McQueen lit a cigarette, cupping it in his hand to shield it from the strong wind that was blowing. He eyed the other strangely. 'You mean, do I believe that Cameron and his associates fell foul of something supernatural?' He shook his head fiercely and took a drag from his cigarette. 'No, of course not. I don't buy that as an explanation. Something undoubtedly did happen, but I'm certain it didn't have anything to do with ghosts or demons. Five people cooped up together in a deserted building in the middle of nowhere — all it takes is for one of them to go mad. Kills everyone in their sleep, one by one, disposes the bodies somewhere they'll never be found and then makes good their escape. Or maybe, two of them working together. That'd be easier. Now clearly, I don't know just why they would do something as despicable as that, but people being people it's not out of the scope of possibility as an explanation. To me, it sounds far more feasible than bringing in the supernatural.'

The ferry was now fast approaching the small harbour where they would be disembarking. Several small cottages dotted the coastline and seagulls cried and circled overhead. After ensuring that they had their rucksacks with them they headed downstairs and waited for the announcement from the captain to instruct them that it was all clear to get off the ferry. When it came, they were the first in the queue to walk down the metal gangplank where they were somewhat surprised to find Mrs. Campbell waiting for them. She was accompanied by two men: a stocky, middle-aged man with a short white beard who from his attire was clearly a priest, and a younger man who bore some resemblance to her.

'Welcome to Islay,' greeted Mrs. Campbell. She gestured to her companions. 'May I introduce my brother-in-law, Father Archie Campbell, and my son, James.'

For a moment McQueen was lost for words. He had not expected there to be others involved in this investigation although he saw no reason why their presence should complicate things. Indeed it could make things easier, providing they knew what they were letting themselves in for. After making his greetings, he and Forsyth followed them to their car.

'So just what are our plans now?' asked McQueen, unslinging his rucksack and handing it over to James Campbell, who had opened the car boot.

'From here, in about half an hour's time, we'll catch the Feolin Ferry over to Jura. Then it's just a relatively short drive along the only road until we get to the point where we have to head off across country. If the weather stays reasonable it should take us about three hours to get to the house,' answered Eleanor Campbell.

*   *   *

McQueen shivered and turned up the collar of his coat as he stood beside the parked car and gazed out at the desolate moorland before him, the dark grey masses of the three mountains barely visible in the low cloud, which threatened

113

to descend and engulf everything. He shivered at something more than just the coldness of the early afternoon air. It was as though an invisible, clinging mist had seemed to rise up out of the ground beneath his feet, bathing him in an aura of impending horror. With an effort, he told himself fiercely that he had to forget that, to keep his mind on the job that lay ahead, and that somewhere out there on the other side of the island there was a ruined house that kept its own mysteries.

A chill light drizzle began to fall.

'*God!* What a place.' Forsyth tightened his bootlaces and then hoisted his rucksack onto his shoulders.

'It's fairly inhospitable, I agree,' commented James. Like the others, he was outfitted in a large raincoat and both he and Archie carried rucksacks as well. 'How my father persuaded the others to come out to this godforsaken place I don't know.'

Tightening a strap on his rucksack, McQueen strode over to join him. 'Did he really believe that the most haunted place in Britain was out here? I'd have thought somewhere like Edinburgh Castle or Highgate Cemetery would've been more his kind of thing.'

'Cameron did indeed think that the place we're going to was the most haunted,' answered Eleanor, before her son could answer.

McQueen glanced upwards, noting that the drizzle had now turned to a cold rain. 'Might be best if we waited in the car until this rain's stopped.'

'Depending on how long the rain's going to last we might not make the house before nightfall, and the path's hard enough to find in daylight,' reasoned Archie in his thick, gruff accent. 'No. I think we'd better head off now, rain or no rain.'

With no further talk, they set off across the bleak, uncompromising landscape, their boots squelching through the thick, peaty sludge of the barely discernible path. After about a mile the path degenerated into nothing more than a trail and in the gathering mist it became increasingly difficult for them to stick to it. The atmosphere had now become oppressive, cold and damp and it did not take long for the imagination to run riot.

Half-formed, tenebrous images seemed to lurk just on the periphery of McQueen's vision, leading him to think that there were things out there, unfriendly things which even now were observing their progress with a malign intent. The mist had become thicker, almost suffocating, the only sounds that of the occasional curse and splash from one of the others. As they progressed through the murk and the gloom the notion that perhaps this was not one of his better ideas came to his mind, and that despite what he had said to Forsyth about enduring the hardships for the sake of fame perhaps it would be best to turn back whilst that still remained an option.

With some measure of inner resolve, he took a hold of himself and trudged on, the ghost-like form of James, whom he was following, just visible up ahead.

After the first hour or so the conditions deteriorated further so that, at least as far as McQueen was concerned, it seemed as though the very elements themselves were conspiring in an attempt to drive them back. A strong wind had now picked up, ice-cold fingers clawing at exposed skin and stabbing sadistically through their waterproofs. With it came an almost horizontal rain that drove at them with a vengeance that seemed born of an elemental fury.

The sky darkened with each passing minute and ill-looking black clouds now replaced the ubiquitous greyness.

A cold sweat trickled down McQueen's spine; an iciness somewhat colder than the rain. On several occasions he was convinced that he heard hideous wails on the wind as though nature itself had become corrupted and had now found some fell voice with which to shriek at them, to warn them perhaps of an impending doom. The ground became soggier, the going more treacherous as deep pools of standing surface water now lay all around and one wrong step would result in an immediate drenching from which hypothermia could easily develop.

The others cursed and struggled on, each absorbed in their own thoughts and nightmares regarding where they were going.

They stopped briefly for a cheerless break, sipping from their flasks and devouring their packed lunches before setting off once more, hoping against hope that they were still heading in the right direction. In the thick fog it was now nigh on impossible to be certain and McQueen dreaded to think what would happen to them if they were to become hopelessly lost out here, for he did not think that there were any adequate search and rescue teams based on the island. Similarly, at least as far as he and Forsyth were concerned, neither of them possessed any appropriate survival knowledge nor, more importantly, had they informed anyone else of where they were going. The latter was an unsettling thought that, unwillingly, plagued his brain for the remainder of the trek.

Thus it was with some relief that, just as darkness was encroaching, James let out a jubilant cry that he could see the house up ahead.

At first McQueen could see nothing through the veil of water that curtained off his immediate surroundings. Then, spectrally, the ruined cottage just seemed to materialise out of the fog before him.

★   ★   ★

By torchlight, they began sifting through the detritus and rubble, stooping occasionally to take a look under many of the heaps of contorted woodwork and jumbled heaps of bricks. What remaining furniture there was lay mostly wrecked and decaying: a bookcase devoid of books against one wall and a few splintered chairs. It was clear that someone had been here, certainly within the last few years, for there were small piles of cigarette butts of a brand McQueen knew to have been only released relatively recently. When he had questioned Mrs. Campbell, she told him that her husband had been a non-smoker, however they could have belonged to members of his team or indeed to the police who had searched the place after the disappearance.

After an hour or so of fruitless ransacking, they decided to camp up — McQueen, Forsyth and Father Archie

119

Campbell setting up base in the ruined main room, whilst Eleanor and her son retired to one of the small side rooms, one which had clearly served as a bedroom of some description.

Outside, the wind and the rain battered without mercy at the derelict building as though trying to outdo each other in terms of ferocity. Despite their hasty, patchwork attempts to provide shelter and make the place somewhat habitable the interior was cold, the atmosphere lugubrious.

'So what do you think happened here, Father?' McQueen asked as he unrolled his sleeping bag and looked for somewhere comfortable to lay it down.

'The Devil's work,' came the gruff reply. 'What else could it be?'

'Would you care to be more specific?'

'I always told Cameron that no good would come of his meddling with things which are best left alone. But would he listen? No! All the time he said he needed to have the proof to substantiate his beliefs. I repeatedly told him that faith should be enough — but alas, it was clearly not enough for him and for those other misguided fools who followed him out here.'

'So I take it you think something unnatural happened here?' asked Forsyth from where he sat, shining the torch all around, making the grotesque shadows dance like wraiths.

'Without doubt. It's one of the main reasons why I agreed to accompany Eleanor. There's evil here. I can sense it. It lives in the very bricks and timbers of this old house. When it shows itself I have all the means necessary to combat it and make it pay for whatever it did to my brother and the others.'

'Are we talking about an exorcism here?' asked McQueen.

'Exactly.' The priest grinned. 'For whereas Cameron sought only to prove the existence of such foul things, I believe it is my duty to permanently destroy such Satanic entities. As I said, I have come prepared. Crucifix. Holy water. Bible. Communion wafers.'

'What are you — some kind of vampire hunter?'

'No. Simply a humble servant of God. One on a crusade to stamp out the Dark and restore the Light to its true brilliance.'

'And what if nothing happens?' said McQueen. 'What if we just end up spending a couple of miserable, cold and wet nights in this deserted shell of a cottage — what then?'

'Ah, but that won't happen. You see it's my aim to draw out whatever evil resides here. Tonight, at the stroke of midnight, I'll conduct a séance to try and do just that.'

'Wait a minute!' protested McQueen. 'Who mentioned anything about holding a séance? That's completely out of the question and I want no part of it. What a ludicrous idea.' He lit a cigarette, his strong features visible for a moment in the flaring match-light.

'Scared of something?' taunted the priest.

'*Scared?* Of such a stupid thing as a séance? No, I'm not scared, but — '

'But what?'

'Well, it's just that I don't have any

belief in anything like that. I don't see the point.'

'Surely we've got nothing to lose and potentially something to gain,' ventured Forsyth. 'Besides, it'll pass the time,' he added flippantly.

'Yes,' said the priest. 'And perhaps as another incentive, think on this: We may gain an insight into just what happened here on that dismal night over a year ago. If I do manage to contact the spirit world perhaps I can find out what really happened to Cameron.'

McQueen had not factored anything like this into his plan of operations. But he might as well humour the man, and besides, he thought it highly likely that Eleanor, who was paying for his services, would want him to participate. So disagreeing would be counter-productive. Later on, after the séance had failed, he might be able to work the conversation round to his theory that one or more members of Cameron's ill-fated team had gone berserk and murdered the others. In the shadowy light, he could see from his watch that it had just gone nine o'clock,

123

so that left nearly three hours in which to get some rest in readiness for midnight and whatever insanity that might bring.

* * *

The exhaustion from the three-hour trudge across the island struck McQueen with a fierce suddenness, dragging him off into a dark slumber as soon as he climbed into his sleeping bag. Almost instantly he was struck by a terrible plethora of dark mental images, each nightmare worse than the one before. Horrible, grinning skull-like faces swam into view before melting away into a swirling mass of blighted wickedness. Surreal, unnatural beings, neither man-like nor animal-like, danced crazily through his silently screaming mind, insane shapes which seemed to fold and unfold before him.

And then, it seemed no sooner had he drifted off into a troubled sleep than he was awakened by James.

'It's getting close to midnight. My mother was hoping that you'd join her and my uncle.'

'What?' asked McQueen groggily, temporarily unsure of his surroundings.

'They're planning on holding a séance in the next room. I can't say that I'm all in favour of the idea but there we are. I don't approve and I don't think it'll help in finding my father.'

Everything rushed back, colliding inside McQueen's brain like a dark tide battering at a sea wall. 'Yes. I must have drifted off for an hour or so.'

'More like three hours,' commented Forsyth, entering the abandoned room. The light from his torch made everything seem frightening and insubstantial shadow-shapes seemed to slink away from the beam of light as though possessed of some sentient quality. 'I guess that hike across the island must've really taken its toll on you.'

McQueen got out of his sleeping bag and followed the others into the adjacent room. A small wooden table had been set up, around which five chairs had been placed. Eleanor and Archie Campbell were already seated, clearly awaiting their arrival.

'When you're ready,' said the priest,

gesturing to the others to sit down in the vacant chairs. Once they had taken their seats he continued: 'Let us all link hands whilst I try and reach out to the spirit world.'

They linked hands as instructed. In his left, McQueen held Eleanor's delicate, long-fingered hand and in his right he grasped Forsyth's. Inwardly, he could not help but think that he was being a gullible fool for even considering participating in this occult nonsense. He had come out here in order to conduct a rigorous and methodical search for any evidence pertaining to the disappearance of Cameron Campbell and his team and now, here he was, gathered around a table joining in with their mumbo-jumbo! He would have to see about asking for extra pay as compensation for this insult to his common sense.

'Is there anyone out there?' intoned the priest. 'Does anyone care to tell us what happened here?' He asked his questions with a quiet deliberation.

McQueen grimaced, his face a portrait in sceptical annoyance. Of course there were people there — themselves.

'Cameron. Are you there, brother?'

'Look, this is getting — ' complained McQueen, getting ready to rise from his chair.

'Wait.' Eleanor threw him a sharp glance.

The room was suddenly very still. All sound ceased abruptly, as if someone had drawn a thick, impenetrable curtain across everything. Utter silence. A finger of ice traced strange patterns along the muscles of McQueen's back. His skin itched and crawled as though a thousand ants were creeping across it.

'Cameron, can you hear me?' In the dim torchlight the priest's face was half-bathed in shadow, giving it a sinister and slightly demonic look.

McQueen felt Eleanor's grasp on his hand tighten, her nails threatening to dig into the flesh of his palm. An eerie atmosphere crowded around them and the temperature dropped noticeably so that he was shocked to see that his breath was now steaming. A long moment passed. There was a low ringing in his ears now and somewhere, at the very edge of his vision, he detected a growing brightness coming from the corner of the room. He clenched his mouth shut to keep his teeth from shaking.

Within the darkness, in the corner of the room, a greenish, dense fog began to gather. The fog began to assume human form, condensing and then solidifying into a tangible being — perhaps not a true flesh and blood one, but a being nonetheless. The ghostly face was lined with pain and torment. Its eyes were tinged crimson and sunken, its face etched with deep lines, and its hair was wild and unkempt.

It was the tortured spirit of Cameron Campbell!

'Cameron!' cried Eleanor.

'*You must all flee!*' wailed the spectre. 'There is a dark spirit here. It will destroy you all as it destroyed me. Your only hope resides in the fireplace. *Save my soul and your own lives . . .* ' Its last cry was a bloodcurdling, fading scream from the netherworld, a truly terrifying caterwaul that shook all of them to the marrow, temporarily paralysing them with fear.

128

Then, his warning given, Cameron's spirit was drawn back into whichever dark beyond it had temporarily been summoned from. It was compressed to a single glowing point, before blinking out of existence.

'What the hell was that!?' cried Forsyth, his eyes wild, his hands trembling visibly. Most of the colour had drained from his face.

A gripping terror clutched at McQueen, forcing him to swallow a lump in his throat. He could feel his heart begin to hammer inside his chest like a caged animal and a cold, damp sweat now leaked from his forehead. He could offer no explanation for what had just transpired; no reasoning enabled him to come to terms with what he had just witnessed with his own two eyes. He had known, instinctively, that what he had seen had been real. It was no trickster's hoax or phantasm generated by a troubled mind, for all of the others had seen it too. It had been something that had defied his logical ordering of the world and all within it, something that his practical, pragmatic outlook on life could not accept, and yet it had happened. *He had seen it!*

Father Archie Campbell was the first to regain some semblance of composure. 'It was the doomed soul of my brother. May his spirit rest in peace.' He broke his hold on those seated next to him and, shakily, made the sign of the cross.

'The fireplace — I wonder what he meant by that?' voiced McQueen, turning his gaze to the ancient, half-collapsed hearth. Charred fragments of wood and an overturned coalscuttle rested close to it, but apart from that it looked completely ordinary.

'And what about this dark spirit?' asked Forsyth nervously.

James got up from his seat and strode over to the fireplace. 'There must be something here,' he said, kneeling down in order to examine the ash-strewn contents of the hearth. A moment or two later, the priest and Forsyth got up to assist him.

They searched around the wide hearth, removing the iron-cast grate and checking for any loose bricks that might conceal any hidden cavities or such like.

'Doesn't seem to be — ' Forsyth stopped mid-sentence as there came a loud crash from the main room. It sounded as though someone had dashed the rotting bookcase to the ground.

All eyes turned in the direction of the doorway.

'What was that?' asked Eleanor.

'Damned if I know,' replied McQueen. He found himself being held by thoughts that he had never believed existed in his mind; an almost tangible fear that was making him now believe in things that he had long consigned to the realm of superstition. Savagely, he tried to throw his gaze into the darkness of the doorway, to try and see whatever may be lurking beyond the shadowy opening. He stood rigid, his heart thudding within his chest.

'We'd better check,' said James, his voice tinged with uncertainty. Hesitantly, he advanced towards the doorway, directing his torch beam in front of him, holding it as though it were a talisman capable of keeping the things of the Dark at bay.

'I'm with you, lad.' Gripping his

crucifix, the priest went first, venturing through the shadow-filled doorway. The rest followed.

The room beyond was much as they had left it only minutes before with one noticeable and horrible exception. An exception that shocked and stunned them all so that for the best part of a minute there was utter silence as they stood gawping, shaking, unable to react as fear paralysed them, gripped them and froze them to the spot.

In the torchlight, written on the nearby wall in what looked like dripping blood was:

I'M GOING TO GET YOU!

It was McQueen who was the first to break free from the hypnotic hold the grim lettering had on them. 'Right. I've seen enough. That writing wasn't there a few moments ago and none of us could have done it. This place *is* haunted. Let's get our stuff together and get the hell out of here.'

'Too right,' agreed Forsyth, staring around him, his eyes wide. 'That's enough for me. We should never have tried that stupid séance.' He moved towards his sleeping bag. 'I'm not staying here a moment longer. This place gives me the heebie-jeebies.'

'This *is* blood,' said James, after testing the viscous red liquid with his fingertips.

'That does it! Get the equipment packed up as quickly as you can. Then we're getting out of this house of horrors.' McQueen turned to Eleanor. 'Sorry about all this, but I hope you understand this goes far beyond what I'd bargained for. If you'd all take my advice you'd leave too.'

'What makes you think you can leave?' asked the priest.

'*What?*'

'I said, what makes you think you can leave?' The priest fixed the private investigator and his assistant with steely eyes. 'Maybe this 'dark spirit' that Cameron warned us about won't let us.'

'That's rubbish.' Hastily, Forsyth crammed his camping gear into his rucksack. He hoisted it onto his shoulders and stomped over towards the front door. All eyes watched him as he turned the handle and opened it.

A strong, cold gust of wind and rain blasted forth but nothing untoward occurred.

'See,' said Forsyth. He closed the door and turned to McQueen. 'Come on, let's get out of here. I'd much rather traipse across ten miles of wilderness than stay a moment longer in this hellish place.'

Once McQueen had all of his gear packed the two of them stood by the door, ready to go and face the elements.

'Are you sure about this?' asked Eleanor, concernedly. She herself was in two minds about leaving, but whilst there remained the slim chance of discovering something about her missing husband she felt compelled to remain. She was scared, more so than she had ever been, but she felt some level of reassurance knowing that Father Archie and her son were with her.

'Damn sure,' said McQueen. He gestured to Forsyth. 'Come on, let's go. If we can get back to the road then — ' He was interrupted by a door slamming shut somewhere along the small corridor that led to the partially destroyed kitchen.

'That's it. I'm out of here.' Forsyth

opened the front door and stepped out into the pitch-blackness, his torch illuminating little but dense shadow. No sooner had he done so than the door slammed shut behind him as though blown by a terrible squall.

'What the hell?' yelled McQueen. He reached for the handle and tried to open it. It was held tight as though some fiendish strength on the outside was keeping it shut.

Then came the screams; awful, blood-curdling cries that hinted at some evil beyond mortal comprehension. And still, despite McQueen's desperate attempts, the door would not yield.

Now they were one down and trapped.

★   ★   ★

For the past ten minutes McQueen had sat on his rucksack, slumped and shivering by the far wall, unable to fully take in the fact that they were now at the mercy of powers beyond his wildest nightmares. Despite repeated attempts to open the front door it now seemed that escape was impossible — not that any of them had the desire to venture outside after hearing the soul-wrenching screams of Forsyth. The windows could have been broken down and in some places escape could have been gained via clambering through the wrecked spaces in the roof, but none had even considered them.

'Perhaps we should search the fireplace again,' suggested Eleanor, her words cutting through the dark melancholy that had now fallen about them.

Checking his watch, McQueen was surprised to find that it was only twenty-five minutes past midnight. It had seemed as though time had become distorted, detached almost from the bizarre reality in which he now found himself. Shaking his head from side to side, he tried in vain to accept that something truly hideous and undoubtedly gruesome had befallen Forsyth. Just what? Well that was something he tried not to think about.

All around them the dilapidated house creaked and groaned, the sound of the storm outside adding to the sense of overall horror and isolation.

'Let's go back into the other room,' said the priest. 'It's clear that there's no more we can do for our friend who went outside. Perhaps if we can find whatever it is that Cameron told us about we may find a means of defeating this evil.'

With no further words, they retreated into the other room, whereupon James started a more intense search of the fireplace. After a few minutes during which both he and the priest had dismantled the surrounding structure it became abundantly clear that nothing was going to be found around the exterior.

'There's nothing here,' said the priest. 'Nothing at all.'

'I'll see if there's anything inside.' With that, James stooped low and, torch in hand, squeezed into the narrow flue so that he was now invisible to those outside from the knees up.

McQueen could hear the sounds of scrabbling coming from inside and he watched as a heap of soot and dust fell from within and piled around the young man's feet. He heard a cough and, after a few seconds, a dislodged brick tumbled into the hearth along with the shattered remains of a small, brown earthenware pot and some other small bits and pieces. 'What's that?' he cried.

Then, before any of them could react there came a horrendous scream from somewhere close by. And then, suddenly, James was hauled off the floor.

'Oh my God!' Eleanor screamed.

The priest made a desperate grab at his nephew's feet, to try and pull him back. He caught hold of one boot and it came off in his hand. And then, screaming, legs kicking frantically, James was wrenched out of sight, dragged up the narrow chimney! His second boot fell into the hearth, landing alongside the pot shards.

'*No!*' Eleanor staggered forward, her eyes staring disbelievingly. She fell into the priest's arms even as McQueen stood staring, unable to help, unable to think clearly.

This was not happening, he tried to tell himself. It was a nightmare, a long and involved nightmare from which he would soon awaken. It was the only explanation his fracturing mind could offer in order to explain all that he had seen since setting foot in this accursed place. He felt as though his scattered wits had been thrown to the dogs; remorselessly shredded and devoured. Something completely outside all of his previous experiences now assaulted him. Whatever this foul thing was that they were now facing, he knew it was an evil thing, spawned out of Hell itself. Fear pulled and tugged at his mind.

Crouching low, McQueen steeled himself to peer inside the hearth but apart from the soot, crumbled brickwork, one boot, bits of pottery and a few spiders there was nothing. No trace of James. 'The fragments of that small pottery jug and those other things. It may be what Cameron was on about.' He stooped to snatch them up before hastily pulling back.

The priest loosed his hold on his sister-in-law, who was now bordering on the inconsolable, tears streaming from her eyes in great wet sobs. James' boot was still in his hand and he stared at it, stupefied. His nephew was gone and this was all that now remained of him.

McQueen examined the contents in his hand with mild revulsion. For amidst the shards of broken pottery was a small wool-like ball of what appeared to be human hair, a few human teeth and some nail clippings. Then realisation dawned. He held in his hand the shattered remnants of a witch-bottle, a vessel used to imprison evil. No doubt Cameron and his team had found it and perhaps unwittingly someone had broken it, unknowingly releasing the evil power that now dwelt here. And as long as the pot was broken the evil could not be contained.

As though that power had now become aware of his understanding it, launched a fresh assault at the house. The doors and the window frames shook with a sudden ferocity. Plaster fell from the ceiling and a mass of bloodied brickwork fell into the hearth.

'In the name of God, I cast you out, foul spirit!' shouted Father Archie, his crucifix held aloft. 'Begone! Leave this place and never return.' His holy declaration resounded around the rubble-filled room. He began to sprinkle holy water around the place. 'By the power invested in me as a servant of God, I cast you out!'

A high-pitched keening scream reverberated around the small room. It was a truly hideous noise; a wild ululation, a banshee's wail that conjured up horrible images and made the remaining three shrink back towards the dark opening of the doorway. The dreadful howl echoed all around, piercing their ears and stabbing into their minds, instilling within them a terrible, brain-numbing sense of dread and despair.

Gritting his teeth, Father Archie fought back against the dark power, chanting the opening words of the Lord's Prayer. Fiercely, he gripped his crucifix, sweat now running in tiny rivulets down his face. Tiny electric pulses were dancing erratically down his arms as he strived to keep the holy symbol aloft, to push back and repulse the demonic entity that now threatened to consume them all.

It was a titanic struggle, and for one dreadful moment McQueen thought that the Dark was going to prevail. But then, with a savage grunt from the priest, the unearthly, cacodemoniacal scream stopped and, temporarily at least, some level of normality returned.

McQueen shook his head in order to clear the insane sound that had assaulted it. For a moment he felt he had been psychically wracked, mentally tortured to the verge of madness. Shaking, he checked his watch, realising that it was now almost ten minutes to one. The witching hour was almost over. Whether that would bring an end to the supernatural malignity directed against them he knew not, but it was a small hope he had to believe in. He doubted whether any of them could survive another night filled with this eldritch insanity.

A deep hush fell over them all.

'Do you . . . do you think it's over?' asked Eleanor, tremulously.

'I don't know,' answered the priest.

'I think you did it,' said McQueen. 'By God, I think you — '

The evil power resumed its attack on them.

Accompanied by a mad cackling laugh, a barrage of bricks was launched malevolently at them. McQueen ducked, but Eleanor did not react quickly enough to avoid getting struck by them. One struck her raised left arm whilst another cracked against her left knee, instantly drawing blood as well as a cry of pain.

A nearby window imploded, showering the priest with flying glass.

'Oh my God!' McQueen rushed forward and grabbed Eleanor, shoving her out of harm's way as a further bout of poltergeist activity brought a large roof beam crashing down, smashing into the floor where she had been only a moment before. Had it struck her she would certainly have been killed.

The three of them withdrew out of the small room. McQueen slammed the door shut. Hastily, they made their way down the small interconnecting passage towards the rear of the cottage.

The sound of cruel, insane cackling pursued them. The walls splintered and cracked. Great ragged zigzags appeared in the coarse stonework.

A hurled brick smacked painfully off McQueen's left shoulder blade. 'Do something!' he screamed hysterically at the priest.

'Quick! In here.' The priest grabbed him and together they stumbled into the small bedroom in which Eleanor and her unfortunate son had set up camp. Archie slammed the door shut. 'I'll try and secure this room,' he said, sprinkling holy water over the door.

Eleanor sat, huddled in an almost catatonic state, her arms wrapped around her knees by her son's rucksack. Her eyes were blank and it was clear, yet not entirely surprising, that something within her mind had finally snapped.

A loud thump smacked against the door.

'Can we defeat this thing?' asked McQueen. 'I've got the pieces from the witch-bottle but I don't see what good — '

'That's it,' said the priest. 'If we can contain the personal items belonging to this fiend, this witch, then we may be able to trap its spirit. We'd be able to force it into a physical form. Only then would we be capable of truly destroying it.'

'Is there anything we can — '
McQueen's searching eyes were drawn to the small thermos flask lying by the rucksack. 'That flask! We'll use that.' He rushed over and snatched it up, emptied out the dregs of tepid coffee and, after a reassuring nod from the priest, delicately dropped the hair, the teeth and the nail clippings inside.

'Just to make doubly sure . . .' Archie decanted a splash of holy water into the flask, making the contents within hiss and steam.

The screams and curses in the corridor grew in intensity. The door shook and rattled like an aggressive lunatic in chains. It was thumped repeatedly. The handle turned repeatedly but thankfully the door would not open.

McQueen screwed on the lid and the priest made a small blessing over it.

The screaming stopped abruptly.

For a long moment there was an unearthly silence, the only sounds those of their laboured breathing and the incessant thumping of their hearts. It seemed as though even the storm that had raged outside all night had finally abated.

'Is it over?' McQueen stared at the door as though half-expecting it to crash open in a violent explosion and for some horror born of nightmare to appear. He looked down at the flask in his hand. Was it just his imagination, or did he feel something shift inside? For a moment he thought about magic lamps and trapped djinns. Was there a similarity? He checked his watch. The witching hour was over and with it, he hoped, the terror that had plagued them.

'I think it is.' The priest listened at the door. Nothing. Slowly, he turned the handle. The door opened a few inches, then met with resistance as though something on the floor was blocking it. He pushed harder and —

In the light cast from his torch, there, lying on the hard stone at his feet, were the grisly, ragged remains of some withered being. It was partially desiccated, the limbs and much of the skull-like face decayed and worm-eaten. Filthy, tangled greying hair, crawling with ticks, sprouted from the head. A crude burial gown was draped around it. One skeletal hand was on the door handle. *It was the corpse of Aggie McSweeney, dead for over a hundred years!*

The Devil's Horseman

Clive Underwood didn't believe in the ghost — but it believed in him.

'Well, seeing as you've decided to stay the night, least I can do is warn you about the ghost.'

'Ghost?' Clive Underwood's eyebrows rose.

'Aye.' The landlord settled himself down in the chair opposite. 'This pub's old, you see. Very old. Some historian bloke a few years ago told me that he'd traced it in some book or other to the mid-fourteenth century. I don't know if it goes that far back but it was certainly used as a staging post and a coach-house during the sixteenth and seventeenth centuries. Anyhow, it's said that old places sometimes retain old memories, and a place like this, well, I bet if the walls could talk they'd be able to tell a tale or two. You may be wondering where it got the name, 'The Devil's Horseman', now that's an interesting — '

'Any chance of getting served?' called out a belligerent voice from the bar.

'Be with you in a minute, Derrick.' The garrulous landlord got to his feet. 'I'll tell you some more of the story once I've served this gentleman.' He went behind the bar and poured a drink. The landlord and his regular were soon gossiping away, moaning about the weather and cursing the price hikes that the new government had introduced.

Underwood took in his surroundings. He was seated in a comfortable snug, a welcoming fire burning in the wide hearth. The walls were decorated with countless old-fashioned horse-brasses and beer mats. There was a small glass-fronted cabinet over to his left in which were housed several trophies, no doubt won by the pub's darts or cribbage teams.

He turned his attention to the three men. The landlord was a dumpy, bespectacled man, probably in his mid-sixties, with a balding head and a cheery grin. The locals were both old, perhaps closer to eighty in age; the one standing at the bar getting his drink was thin and gaunt, the seated one small and bearded. Something in the smaller man's facial features and the way his eyes were constantly moving, darting around in his head, made Underwood think of hamsters.

Outside, he could hear the rain lashing at the lead-lined windows and he silently cursed once more the fact that he had ended up here in the first place. For he had set out across the Peak District from his home in Preston with the intention of visiting his brother in Sheffield, a journey he had made dozens of times. On this occasion, however, he had fallen foul of an uncanny number of road diversions that had forced him out onto ever more minor roads until he had been forced into unknown territory, back roads that were seldom travelled along. Then had come the puncture.

He must have walked two and half miles or so through the rain until his weary feet had brought him to the hamlet of Stickleborough. It had been dark when he had arrived, so all he had been able to distinguish apart from the single public house on the hill had been a shadowy collection of slate-roofed houses, half a dozen or so, certainly no more than that. Neither the landlord nor the two other men inside had cars, so they had been unable to drive him to a garage. There wasn't a phone either.

Silently cursing his ill luck, Underwood sighed and reached for his pint. At least the ale was good; some local beer he'd never sampled before. There was an opened packet of cheese and onion crisps before him into which the landlord had placed a pickled egg, informing Underwood that it was a delicacy in these parts and that, seeing as they didn't serve food, he might as well make the most of it.

Wiping his hands on a bar towel, the landlord walked over and took his seat again. 'What were we talking about? Oh aye, the ghost.'

'Before you go on, I must tell you that I don't really believe in things like that.' Underwood took a sip from his beer. 'In fact, I'd even go as far as to say I've never believed in anything supernatural — ghosts, flying saucers, the Loch Ness Monster. I think it's all a load of hogwash.'

'You're entitled to your view, of course,' said the landlord. 'But there are things that go on here nobody's ever been able to explain. In fact, there was a team from York University that came here about three years ago in order to carry out some kind of investigation.' He called to his regulars. 'You remember that, don't you Derrick?' he shouted.

The old codger looked over from where he and his pal sat, engrossed in a game of dominoes. 'What's that?' It was clear he was hard of hearing.

'I'm telling our friend here about the ghost.'

'What?'

'The ghost!' shouted the landlord.

'Are you still rabbiting on about your bloody ghost? You're wasting your time on the wrong kind of spirits.' Derrick and his bearded pal broke into a fit of laughter and returned to their game.

A wry smile creased Underwood's mouth.

The landlord waved a dismissive hand. 'Ah, take no notice of them.' He leaned further across the table. 'What them two don't know is what happened on the last night of that investigation. Three of them, including the professor or whatever he was, chose to stay in the room at the end of the corridor. They gave strong orders that no matter what was heard nobody was to open the door of that room, either to go in, or to let them out, until morning.'

A tiny germ of apprehension crept into the pit of Underwood's stomach. It was a dim, nervous feeling, a very slight trembling that now crept like a rising shadow up his spine. Admittedly, he didn't believe in ghosts, but that didn't mean that hearing tales of them didn't bring a certain unease. It was all to do with setting and environment, he told himself. For no doubt the story he was going to be told would be deemed laughable if related in a busy café in town but here, in this isolated, storm-battered, virtually empty public house, its horror and indeed believability would be magnified substantially. It was all down to atmosphere, he told himself.

The landlord continued, 'And so, they went in and locked the door behind them. I then left them to it. Now I don't know what they got up to in there and if there's a God in Heaven hopefully I'll never find out, but I think it may've been a séance or something like that. For half the night I heard nothing, my room being at the far end of the corridor, nearer the stairs. Then I was woken about three in the morning by an almighty banging. Then came the shouts. I threw on a dressing gown and rushed out, flicking on all of the lights. It was the door! They were thumping on the door, screaming to get out. Screaming they were!'

'But you said they had the key. Why didn't they use it?' asked Underwood.

'I shouted that at them. 'You've got the key,' I told them. 'You can open the door.' They shouted back something about: 'He's got it now. He won't let us out!''

'Who's 'he'?' Underwood looked confused.

'The Highwayman, I assumed. The ghost.'

Despite his scepticism, a shiver ran through Underwood. Perhaps it was something to do with the level of sincerity the landlord brought to his storytelling or, more than likely, the environment — combined with the growing realisation that the room in question would no doubt be the very same one he would be staying in. A sensation of sick apprehension grew within him. He was beginning to sweat, the pleasant warmth from the fire now no longer comfortable. Before he knew it, he was feeling a little scared. Of nothing — of everything.

'I stood there, looking at the door, not knowing what to do. I'd given my word, you see, that I wouldn't open it and they'd paid good money up front in order to do their bit of ghost-hunting, so the last thing I wanted to do was break my promise and see if I could find the spare key in order to let them out. But their screams were becoming wild and unbearable, terrible to listen to. By this time two of the other students who had been kipping down here in the snug rushed up. Like me, they didn't know what to do. Suddenly, it fell silent. I could see the fear on the faces of those students who were in the corridor with me. I knocked several times. Nothing.'

There was a moment's pause. A drawn-out hesitation that made Underwood think that perhaps his informant was intentionally spinning out his yarn in order to create the right level of suspense. He took another sip of beer.

'Well, I assumed that things had quietened down, got back to normal. And that's when I heard the key turn in the lock.'

Underwood thought that the atmosphere inside the snug changed; became colder. For whereas only minutes before he had been uncomfortably hot, he now felt a damp chill in his bones. He found it hard to relax and digest this ghost story in the way it should have been taken, with a laugh and a dismissive shake of the head. It was all nonsense, he tried to tell himself.

'I stepped back, away from the door, not knowing what was going to come out. It was the professor. The look on his face will haunt me for the rest of my days, I'm sure. He muttered something and shambled towards me, all grey and deathly; hollow-eyed. Those two students that had accompanied him came out next and I knew then that they'd seen or experienced something in that room. Something had scared them half to death, of that I was certain. Once they were out, the professor gave me the key, and told me to lock the door and never open it again. They had packed up within ten minutes and set off into the cold and the rain, on foot, even though they had a bus coming to collect them in the morning. They refused to spend another minute here.'

Underwood finished his pint. He put the glass down on the table. 'And I take it this is the room I'll be spending the night in?' He did his best to hide any fear there may have been in his voice. The rational part of his mind tried to dominate the darker side; tried to make him believe that perhaps these psychic investigators had made a hoax out of the whole thing, perhaps in order to generate sensationalism to justify their own undertakings. Yes, no doubt that was the explanation — nothing more than acting.

'It's the only spare room I have.' There was a slightly mischievous smile on the landlord's face. 'But I think you knew that anyway.'

'I had a feeling.'

'You could always bed down here. I could see about — '

'That won't be necessary. I told you, I don't believe in ghosts. I will have another pint though.' Underwood waited until the landlord had returned with a second ale. 'So who's this highwayman?'

'Robert Darcy, also known as 'Black Robert' and 'The Devil's Horseman'. He were a scourge of these parts three hundred years ago. A highwayman with a heart of darkness. Don't be thinking of any of this 'stand and deliver', Dick Turpin nonsense. Darcy was a vicious robber and a killer. I reckon he'd be classed a massmurderer by today's standards as he must've killed over twenty, maybe thirty people. Rumour had it he was in league with a coven of witches and that he'd sold his soul to the Devil in order to make him uncatchable.'

'I take it he was caught though?'

'Caught? In a manner of speaking, I suppose. The authorities laid an ambush for him. They set up a decoy carriage filled with armed riflemen somewhere on the road just outside. Darcy, thinking it an easy target, tried to rob it whilst some of his gang were still in here, deep in their cups. There was a bit of a shoot-out but he were clearly outnumbered. The soldiers caught him and clapped him in the gibbet that used to hang on the wall at the back of the pub. One story tells that he spent days there, pelted and abused by the families of his victims before he and his gang were taken to Sheffield where they were executed. An even weirder story, and one that that professor from York certainly believed, was that for some reason or other they dragged him into the cellar, half-beat him to death and then bricked him up alive in a secret room. Now I don't know for sure what exactly happened that night all those years ago but I do know that on nights like this, when the wind howls on the moors and the moon's full and bright, you can sometimes hear faint sounds like tortured screams from the cellar.'

'Spooky.' Underwood swallowed a nervous lump in his throat. He was beginning to think that the landlord was trying to dissuade him from staying here at all. All this talk of wraiths and spectres — it was hardly gossip conducive to make him want to spend the night here. Now if he'd said: 'The bed's lovely and comfortable and I'll make you a hearty breakfast in the morning as well as see about getting someone in the village to give you a lift into the nearest town'. . .

Instead, he went on, his topic of conversation becoming more ghoulish: 'Aye, it is that. I daren't go down there unless I have to. There's a chill feeling you get. As though something's watching from the shadows, ready to pounce. And I've heard other things as well. A terrible horse neighing outside at all hours, day and night. But of course when I go to look, there's nothing there. Nor are there any horses within miles of this place. Then there's the footsteps. Not normal footsteps mind you, but the sound of booted feet. Jangling, spurred, booted feet that walk the stairs and corridors, treading on the boards overhead. Malcolm over there claims to have seen something out on the road one night not so long ago. A pale, fleshy thing, lit up in the moonlight. He refuses to talk about it anymore. And as for the long-haired, naked thing Derrick saw one night, dancing on the roof, howling at the moon — '

'Do you actually want me to stay here?' Underwood came right out with it. 'I mean, forgive me for asking, but you seem to be doing your utmost to try and convince me otherwise. Look, I've told you I don't believe in ghosts or any other things that go bump in the night, but you really seem to be trying to make me seek alternative accommodation. Are you trying to purposefully scare me away?'

'Not at all, sir.' The landlord shook his head. 'I'm merely warning you. I'm also covering my own back as it were. You see, if the worse should happen — '

'What are you talking about?'

'I'm just saying that if the worse should happen, Derrick and Malcolm there will vouch for me when I say I tried to warn you. That's all.'

'Very well, consider your conscience clear. You've told me and I still plan on sleeping here. It's not as though I've much choice now, is it?'

'I guess not.'

Underwood checked his watch, noting that it was now ten minutes to ten. 'Right. Well, it's getting late. As soon as I've finished this pint would you be so good as to show me to my room?'

* * *

Underwood waited outside in the dimly-lit corridor as the landlord fumbled with the key in the door lock. At first, he thought the man was going to have trouble opening the door, that perhaps he was using the wrong key, but then the lock clicked and he turned the handle, opening the door. It creaked on un-oiled hinges, the sound grating on his ears.

For a moment, the landlord was hesitant to enter. He merely stood there at the threshold gazing into the shadowy darkness. With a deep breath, he mustered his courage and stepped inside. Reaching to his left, he found the light switch and flicked it down.

Nothing happened.

He flicked it up and down.

Still nothing.

'Great. No lights. This just keeps getting better.' Contemptuously, Underwood shook his head.

'Maybe the bulbs have gone. I'm afraid I haven't got any spares so I'll nip downstairs and get some candles. I know I've got a box of them somewhere.'

Underwood stood, waiting whilst the landlord went to fetch the candles. He gazed uneasily into the dark interior of the room, its furnishings nothing more than barely discernible outlines in the poor light that spilled in from the corridor. Narrowing his eyes, he tried to throw his vision into the darkness, to pick out details. There was a large bed, a chair, a cabinet —

Something moved.

His heart lurched into his mouth. Paralysed by the suddenness and the utter surprise, he pulled back, his eyes wide, staring. There was nothing there, he tried to tell himself, just a figment of his overwrought imagination — a shadow phantom no doubt brought about by all the talk of the ghostly highwayman. He jumped at the approaching sound of the landlord.

'Got some candles. Should be enough to make the place bright, and, dare I say, cheery.'

Underwood grinned. He hadn't stayed at many places over the course of his forty-seven years of life, but none of those he had stayed at came close to being as unusual as this place. And the same went for its owner. He was an oddball, without doubt. Perhaps he had lived in this relative isolation for too long, his only company those two old codgers downstairs.

Matches were struck and then, candle in hand, the landlord ventured inside the alleged haunted room.

Now that he could see it better, Underwood was mildly surprised and pleased with what he saw. For this was no crumbling, cobweb-festooned garret with bats hanging from the beams or evil-eyed portraits on the walls. Instead it was a relatively cosy-looking bedroom. It was quite tastefully furnished; nothing extravagant but certainly adequate for one night. And it would only be for one night, of that he was sure. In the morning, he'd sit and wait by the road and flag down another passing motorist, hitchhike into the nearest town in order to find a garage or somewhere that had a telephone so that he could contact his brother.

The landlord strategically positioned a few more candles, illuminating the room further. 'The bathroom's out the door, second on the left,' he said, lighting a further one. 'Right, I'll leave the other candles and the matches here in case you need them.'

'Thanks.'

'Well, I wish you good night. I'd ask you what cereals you'd like for breakfast, but something tells me, well — ' The landlord stepped out into the corridor and shut the door.

'Good God,' muttered Underwood. That man really did think that this room was haunted and that something sinister would happen to him during the night. It was just his luck to end up in this creepy place with its equally creepy owner who would certainly not be winning any gold stars for hospitality. In spite of all that he had been told that evening and the warning the other had been at pains to deliver, he still steadfastly refused to believe in any unnaturalness associated with this place, this room in particular.

Dimly, at the range of his hearing, he could hear the sounds of the three men downstairs in the bar. Their conversation sounded strangely muffled, far more so than when he had stood outside in the corridor, although this was probably due to the thickness of the door, he reasoned.

In his mind's eye, he could see the landlord downstairs, laughing and joking at his expense. Yes, no doubt he and his cronies were getting real belly laughs, thinking that they had put the fear of God into him with all that ghostly talk. As a stranger in these parts no doubt he was seen as an easy target, someone to ridicule. Well, let them have their laugh. At the end of the day they were the sorry souls stuck out here in the middle of nowhere, whereas he would be leaving in the morning.

An unbidden and unwanted nervous fear suddenly sprang on him as he remembered that movement he thought he had seen in the darkness. In the candlelight, he tried to dismiss it further, to reinforce the notion within his brain that it had been nothing more than his imagination. After all there was nothing here now. And if it had been something it may have been nothing more harmful than a cat. Yes, perhaps that was what he had seen. Maybe it was now cowering in fear under the bed.

He walked over to the bed, crouched down and looked underneath. There was nothing. Ah well, maybe it hadn't been a cat; maybe it had just been his imagination after all. Testing the bed for comfort, he found the mattress to be too hard, and it had but one rather flimsy blanket on it. There was, however, a large armchair in the corner of the room, which looked far more appealing. He went over to it and sat down, sinking into its welcoming softness.

He sat there for a while, listening to the dull sounds from below. If only he had brought a book with him from his car when he had abandoned it in the lay-by, then he could spend an hour or two reading. Looking around him, he could see no books or any other kind of reading material. Resignedly, he closed his eyes and started to doze, his chin dropping onto his chest, his tired eyes drooping. He thought he heard a door slam — probably the two locals leaving. Then he was nodding, fatigue pulling him down into a disturbed slumber.

* * *

The candles had burned low by the time Underwood awoke. His sleep had been filled with troubling dreams which were now mercifully dissolving from his mind, so that now, mere seconds after waking up, he couldn't remember specifics. That they had been unpleasant he was sure, a fact also supported by the sheen of cold perspiration that dampened his body. He checked his watch. It was now twenty minutes past midnight.

Rising from the chair, he stretched his limbs. It was then that he noticed it. A slight man-shaped outline on the bed where someone — or something — had been lying. After rubbing his tired eyes, he stared harder. There it was — a definite indented outline where some pressure had been put on the cover and the mattress. Had he, in his sleep, wandered over and slept there? Only to sleepwalk back to the chair afterwards? It seemed highly unlikely.

Closing his eyes, Underwood counted to ten, breathed deep and looked again. The depression had gone! He was just about to head over to the bed for a closer look when he heard a dull clang as of metal on stone from outside the window.

The sound came again, only this time it was less of a clang, more a metallic rattle, like the winching of a length of thick-linked chain, the kind of thing that raised and lowered drawbridges.

Underwood tried to tell himself that it was only the landlord doing something or other in the yard; perhaps moving heavy, metal beer barrels or closing a gate. Curious, he walked over to the window and peered out.

All was dark. Raising the latch, he forced the window open, bringing in the cold, the wind and the rain. There was nothing there. Then he heard something over to his left, a scraping sound. Just the sound an iron gibbet would make as it swung against a wall. Underwood stood for a moment, not daring to turn his head. Then he quickly glanced to the left. There was nothing there. He breathed out explosively. Just for a moment his heart had seemed to stop. Pulling his head back inside, he laughed nervously. That ghost story had really got to him, he thought.

Looking around the room, he saw the candles were beginning to gutter and started to replenish them from the box left by the landlord. As he lit the third, the first two suddenly died. Frowning, Underwood took out another match and brought it towards a wick. It too blew out instantly and he felt a distinct breeze on his face. He had secured the window and the foul weather outside had died down, but there was a wind picking up in the room. As he spun round to see if the door had come open, all the candles went out at once and he was plunged into darkness. He struggled to contain a shout of alarm and his fingers fumbled for a match. Twice, the struck match failed to catch, but on the third attempt it fired into life and he cupped his hands around it, sheltering the flame as he scanned the room, a growing feeling of panic threatening to overwhelm him. Turning to look at the bed, he saw for a moment a figure, indistinct but visible, lying on it. He had only the briefest glimpse of a bloodstained jacket and a badly bruised face before he ran for the door, frantically turning the key in the lock. To his relief it opened and he fell through into the corridor, gasping for breath and whimpering.

There was a low laugh from the room behind him as he slammed the door shut.

On legs that had turned to jelly, Underwood half-staggered down the short corridor. 'Wake up! Wake up, damn you!' He hammered on the landlord's bedroom door. He had found the light switch in the corridor and the flood of light helped to calm his nerves a little, but there was no way he would stay in that room the rest of the night.

The door opened and the landlord peered out blearily into the corridor.

'What is it? What's wrong?' he asked.

'That room . . . the ghost . . . I can't stay there.' Underwood spoke incoherently.

'Eh? What are you on about?'

'That room *is* haunted. There's something there. I'm going downstairs.'

Before the landlord could reply, Underwood made for the narrow stairs that led down into the bar area. He had to search for a moment or two in order to find the light switch. He flicked it on, instantly bathing the room in brightness. It was as he remembered it but more importantly it was empty, ghost-free.

Quite suddenly he had the desire to get completely away from this place. He wished he had never set foot inside and the need to flee out the door, into the night, to keep walking until he came to somewhere else, almost overwhelmed him. It was an urge that he managed to control and sitting down here, in the light, made him think, once more, that perhaps it had all been nothing more than his imagination. There was no doubt that dark stories engendered dark thoughts.

Nerves tingling, he jumped as he heard

a door opening above him. Then came the creak of floorboards and the sound of footsteps coming down the stairs. A few seconds later, the landlord appeared and he let out a sigh of relief.

The landlord went behind the bar, poured a brandy and came over with it. Presenting it to Underwood, he took a seat opposite. 'I've got some apologising to do,' he said. 'But first, get this down you. It'll make you feel better.'

Underwood took a sip, grimacing somewhat as the raw liquor burnt his throat.

'I am sorry, sir, what with laying on that story about the Highwayman and all. It's something I tell all new guests I get. It's a load of rubbish, you see. A little bit of banter just to give me something to talk about and make this run-down, godforsaken place seem a bit more characterful and colourful than it really is.' The man removed his glasses and gave them a wipe. 'There's no ghost here. Nor was there ever any team of investigators. I just thought to myself one day that a place with a name like 'The Devil's Horseman' should have a ghost, a bit of a reputation, so I made up the story.'

'You — you made it up?'

'Aye, as a joke. But I can see that it's given you a nightmare, and for that I'm truly sorry. I've had dozens of folk stay in that room and none of them have ever seen anything.'

'But I saw something. There was something there.'

'No, sir. It's just your imagination. But if you'd rather stay down here for the night then that's alright by me. I'll get you some blankets and a pillow and — '

'That won't be necessary,' said Underwood tersely. 'I'm awake now and I don't intend to go back to sleep.' He finished his brandy.

'As you please, but the offer's there.' The landlord got to his feet. 'Just remember that there are no ghosts here. I'll see you in the morning.' He made his way back upstairs to his room.

Underwood eased himself into the comfort of his chair.

There was something here, something which if not truly evil was certainly close to it. It was not the evil of voodoo or of

witchcraft, which were said to be prac-
tised in the far distant jungles of Africa
and which were things a man could laugh
at, so long as he didn't believe in the
weird superstitions of the natives. No, this
was something utterly different, subtly more
horrible; terrible, in a manner that was
hard to define. The sensation he had experienced when he had glimpsed the body
on the bed had been like an electric shock
coursing through him.

A riot of half-formed ideas was running
through Underwood's brain. To be told
one thing and then to be told that it had
all been nothing but a pack of lies. And
yet, he had experienced something in that
room. Or had he? Could it be, as the
landlord had said, nothing but his own
imagination, fuelled by the tale the other
had related, which had projected such
images and sounds on to his mind?

Everything should have been sane and
normal now that the myth of the Highwayman had been exposed as fraudulent,
nothing more than fiction created with
the sole intent of scaring him. But instead,
Underwood could feel the presence of

unknown horrors ringing him around, pressing in on all sides, gathering about him in the same way darkness comes creeping out of the far corners of a room whenever a candle burns low.

He tried to shake himself free of whatever power or other was trying to possess him, to make him do things that no clear-thinking individual would dare contemplate. He felt as though he was succumbing to this siren's song, this unearthly force that was now filling his mind with an inner madness.

Everything was very quiet. The storm had abated and as he sat there, alone in the bar, he tried hard to shake away the eerie sights he had seen. He was of half a mind to go and pour himself a second brandy when that silence was broken by the sound of a baleful moan from over to his right. Shaking, he turned to look. There was a door, half-open, beyond which was a corridor which he assumed led to the kitchen.

A chill spread slowly over him as he stood staring, listening, his senses strained to the utmost. The shiver came back. His mind was now floundering like a swimmer caught out of their depths, struggling against a dark undertow of frightening possibilities that his rational, logical brain battled to constrain. Little beads of icy coldness ran down his forehead as, for what seemed a timeless period, he stared transfixed at where the moan had come from.

Nothing emerged from the room beyond and he was about shift his vision when the groan came again, louder this time. What mad impulse made him get him to his feet and head over in order to discover the source of that ghastly sound he didn't know but, upon throwing the corridor door wide, he saw nothing more alarming than a small, untidy kitchen over to his left and another door some ten feet directly in front of him.

It was the door to the cellar.

It slowly swung open.

Trembling, Underwood stood, eyes wide. His mind was a tumult of terrible thoughts and fear was a bubbling sensation in his throat. Deliberately, he forced himself to think of something other than the door to the cellar — the cellar, where the landlord had told him the Highwayman had been bricked up alive. But that was just fabrication, he told himself, trying to get it out of his mind. The landlord had said so. So why was he still scared? Why did he remain unconvinced?

A strange compulsion dragged him forward.

Reaching the cellar door, he stood for a moment, peering down into the damp-smelling darkness. That rational part of his mind told him to step away, to go back into the well-lit bar and stay there till daybreak, keeping all of the lights on, having another drink, get plastered — anything but venture down there.

Obeying a power that he was no longer able to resist, Underwood flicked on the light switch and proceeded carefully downstairs. The boards creaked as he stood on them, his right hand trailing down the wall where paint and stained wallpaper peeled and sloughed off in patches like diseased skin. The reek of damp was mixed with the heady, slightly intoxicating smell of ale and cider.

The cellar was small, lit only by the one

bare bulb. To his right was the ramp leading to the bolted outer door through which barrels were lowered. Many of those barrels were in front of him, various lines and lengths of tubing leading from them to the beer pumps in the bar. Several crates and boxes of unopened bottles lay heaped against the wall to his left.

Every sense strained to the utmost, Underwood stood there for what seemed an eternity, gazing around him. And then he heard it. A whimpering that came from behind the stacked crates. He screamed silently, inwardly, unable to articulate the terror that clutched at his soul. There was a dull, persistent throbbing in his ears and a stabbing at his temples that wouldn't go away. And yet, whereas a sane individual would by now have fled, clambered back up the stairs and perhaps run screaming out of the public house, he found himself captivated by the sounds, unable to function rationally, unable to act as common sense dictated.

Crouching low, he moved towards the crates. The sound was getting louder.

Systematically, he began moving the boxes,

piling them in the centre of the cellar. The wall space beyond was bare, ordinary.

Underwood stepped back, scanning the length of exposed brickwork.

There was a dark tugging at his brain, an external influence that took possession of him. Looking around for something — and yet he had no real idea what — he found himself going back upstairs and into the kitchen. Pulling open a drawer, he found a metal ladle, several knives and half a dozen spoons. Gathering up the kitchen utensils, he then made his way back into the cellar.

He used the ladle first, scooping and chipping away at the surface. The first knife he used snapped but the second proved harder, and he scraped away at the mortar binding the bricks. It was relatively easy going, far easier than he had anticipated, and he seemed to be working now with a certain mechanical efficiency as though he had become but the tool for something far more driven. Using the handle of the ladle, he tapped one of the loosened bricks in. It fell away revealing a dark cavity beyond.

Underwood was working hard now, feverishly chipping at the bricks, widening the aperture. The more he cleared, the easier it became. Within fifteen minutes he had created a gap wide enough to insert his head into.

He peered into the bricked-up room. At first he could see little, just the rubble-strewn floor and the dislodged bricks. Then, as his eyes became accustomed to the gloom, he could discern the outline of something lying on the ground in the far corner.

Eagerly, he began tearing at the wall, widening the breach. Still unable to clearly see whatever it was that lay in the corner, Underwood stepped back, reached up and took down the light-bulb on its length of cable. With this in hand, he went back to the hole.

The thing in the corner was a ragged, man-sized skeleton dressed in a tattered coat and wearing scuffed leather riding boots. Around one ankle, attached to the wall by a short length of rusty chain, was a manacle.

It had to be the long-dead remains of

the Highwayman, Robert Darcy.

An inner voice told Underwood to come closer, that there was nothing for him to fear. He obeyed, clambering into the long-forgotten secret room, the length of cable long enough to permit illuminating the interior. Crouching down, he set about gouging away the brickwork that secured the worn bracket to which the length of manacle had been bolted.

Not once did he stop to think what would happen if the landlord were to appear on the scene. Here, before his very eyes, was the physical evidence to prove the latter's own make-believe. Just how did one explain or come to terms with that? Under different circumstances Underwood would have been dumbfounded, unable to accept any of this.

The knife he was using broke, its blade shattering. A shard slit his hand.

There was no blood!

Underwood stared. Of all the weirdness he had seen and experienced since arriving at the Devil's Horseman, for some reason this was the most inexplicable. Grimacing, he pinched the sliver of metal between his thumb and forefinger of his left hand and plucked it out. Perhaps the wound hadn't been deep enough to draw blood, he told himself.

The unspoken command returned, more urgently, dragging his attention back to the bracket. Using a spoon, he managed to loosen it and, with a tug, he snapped it free.

A green, ethereal mist gathered above the skeleton. It swirled and billowed, thickening, becoming a smoke which solidified into a man-shaped thing; a cruel-faced individual resplendent in a long dark coat and tricorne hat. Shoulder-length black hair, an eye-patch and a roguish goatee beard completed his devilish, rugged good looks.

'Ye've freed me.' The spectre's voice was cold and chilling.

Underwood was speechless. He stood in awe. Then he looked at the spoon in his hand. It was a poor weapon if things turned nasty. A thought crept into his mind as he tried to explain to himself just what this thing could be. Could it be that this 'ghost' had been given some form of semi-existence by the oft repeated story related by the landlord? For, if as some believed, apparitions were but echoes of past events, trapped like photographic images on certain backgrounds, visible only to those receptive enough to see them, then it wasn't too much of a stretch to theorise that ideas and beliefs could do likewise: thoughts made flesh, or ectoplasmic in this case. This didn't quite explain the presence of the skeleton though. Could the landlord have somehow picked up a resonance of this ghost and unwittingly have based his story on forgotten fact?

'Well? Don't ye speak?'

'You're a ghost, aren't you? The ghost of the Highwayman, 'Black Robert'.'

Something remotely resembling a smile creased the wraith's mouth. ''Black Robert'. Aye, that was my name. But tell me, who are ye? I don't recognise yer attire. And what happened to yer head?'

'My head?' Underwood looked confused.

'Yer head.' The ghostly highwayman pointed to the other's forehead.

Underwood touched the place in question, alarmed when he felt the dampness. Worried, he examined his fingertips and saw blood, black and wet. Had he banged his head in his desperate attempt to unearth and liberate the ghost? It was certainly possible.

'Were ye beaten too? Or did ye fall from a carriage?'

'I don't understand what you're talking about.'

'How did ye die, man?'

'*What?! I'm not dead.*'

'Hah! And neither am I.' The ghost threw its head back and laughed. There was a certain malice in its mirth. 'Of course ye're dead, and nearing the end of yer time of influence. I was fortunate; another few minutes and ye couldn't have freed me.'

'But . . . ' Underwood's world crumbled away before him. In a dark flash of memory, he saw his hands frantically grasping at the car's steering wheel as he battled to control it in the storm. The tyres screeched as he skidded, slamming on the brakes. Then came the shattering impact.

A nightmare. It was all a long, involved nightmare. Frantically, he crawled out of the bricked-up room and rushed out of the cellar. At the top, he paused, trying to muster the courage to check his wrist for signs of a pulse. He couldn't bring himself to do it.

More scared than he had ever been in his life, Underwood reeled into the bar. There was a mirror on the wall. With a sense of grave trepidation, he went over to it.

The reflected image was not him. It couldn't be. For the man that stared back at him from behind the thin layer of silver-backed glass was bruised and bloody; deathly, a living corpse, a car crash fatality.

Underwood continued to stare, unbelieving. 'No!' he cried, although no sound came from his lips. He could not, would not accept any of this. How could he be dead? The dead didn't get out of their cars and walk for the best part of an hour through the night before entering a public house in order to find lodgings.

Didn't they? spoke a little voice in his mind. After all, how would he know? How would anyone living know?

No! No! No! He silently screamed.

Woodenly, he staggered out of the bar area and made for the stairs. Taking them slowly, he went up and headed along the corridor to the room at the end. He stood at the threshold and beheld his own dead body lying on the bed.

Insanity overwhelmed Clive Underwood as all outward sensation began to dissipate from him, to pour out of him like water from an upturned vessel. He was fading, disintegrating, becoming incorporeal, his time spent as one of the walking dead almost over. And still, he could not accept what was happening to him. He looked at his hands and saw with stunned horror that they were dematerialising before his very eyes. Then his arms and legs. Then, he disappeared entirely, simply phased out of existence.

* * *

After the landlord had found the bar empty, he went upstairs and looked in the small room where his guest had stayed. There was no one there. Shaking his head in confusion, he went back downstairs and into the kitchen to fix himself some breakfast. He was halfway through his cornflakes when the bell at the front door began to ring.

'Hang on,' he shouted. He went to the door, unlocked it and opened it.

On the front step was one of his locals.

'Morning, Derrick. Bit early for you to be up and about, isn't it?'

'Thought you'd be interested in this. Happened yesterday evening, just down the road at that turning off for Houghton. A terrible black spot for accidents that.' The old man handed his morning copy of the local paper over. On it, printed in bold lettering, was:

MAN KILLED IN CAR TRAGEDY

47-year-old Clive Underwood was pronounced dead at the scene . . .

The landlord found himself unable to read any more. His eyes were focused on the unfortunate's photograph. It was the man who had stayed the night, the one who had been so scared by his tale of 'The Devil's Horseman'. He was temporarily struck dumb, his hands trembling.

'You alright? Looks like ye've seen a

ghost or something.'

'It's him. It's the man who came here last night.'

'What man? There was nobody in 'The Horseman' last night save for you, me and Malcolm.'

'But — ' The landlord stared hard at the other. 'But, surely you saw him? You know, the one we were winding up about the ghost?'

'It were just you, mumbling to yourself over by the fire.' Derrick shook his head. 'I may be a bit deaf but there's nothing wrong with my eyes. You're the one who wears glasses.'

There had to be some confusion, thought the landlord. There had to be, for the alternative was impossible, unthinkable. He stared once more at the photograph of Clive Underwood. It had to be someone else . . .

Of course his true horror was to come when he discovered what lay in the cellar . . .

With the Setting
of the Sun

It was only when the sun set that the ancient standing stone revealed its terrible secret.

'Britain is dotted with strange and peculiar Neolithic archaeological sites, many of which defy true explanation. What I mean is, when you get right down to it, expert interpretation is solely based on the surviving evidence: standing stones, ditches and other features in the landscape. There's no one around from prehistory to talk to and say: 'Excuse me, my good man, but just why did you build this ring of stones and what's it for?'' Professor Arthur Madden took a sip from his hip-flask, the raw whisky stinging his throat and filling his gullet with a warming sensation, chasing away some of the chill of the cold mid-November morning. 'Take this long barrow for instance.' He gestured to the low mound that stood before the small gathered team of students, its entrance flanked by two large flat stones. 'Similar to Wayland's Smithy, it was excavated nigh on a hundred years ago by Pitt Rivers. Many of the artefacts are now in the museum and I'd suggest you all take a good look at them. However, we've got very little to go by other than saying it was clearly used for burial purposes. As I said earlier, there are no written accounts from that remote time to clarify its real purpose, if indeed it had one other than as a repository for the dead.'

The lecture now over, the students spent ten minutes or so crawling inside to examine the cist chambers with torches and walking around the five-thousand-year-old earthwork, chattering to themselves and making notes and diagrams whilst Madden finished his whisky. He drank unashamedly and indeed his fondness for booze was something which had endeared him to many of his students, making him more like one of them than some of the other dusty old fossils, his fellow academics at the university.

He was just about to call time, to get them all back in the minibus, when he saw a green car appear over the distant rise close to the car park some quarter of a mile away where the minibus was parked. The car came to a standstill and a man in a dark coat got out. He was using a walking stick although his walking seemed fine. It surprised Madden that another person should turn up, for not only was it still a relatively early hour of the day, but this place was quite isolated, the closest village several miles distant. What would someone be doing out here?

His thoughts were interrupted when one of his brighter students came over.

'Professor, I read somewhere that there may be a ritual element involved with the spatial distribution of these mounds and tumuli, similar in some way to the positioning of the pyramids at Giza and the Mayan temples, and that there may be an astrological — '

'Astronomical.' Madden wagged a finger. 'There may be an *astronomical* reasoning behind their location. Yes, I too believe that. Although it's less apparent for the positioning of burial mounds, Newgrange aside, as say, for example, stone circles and avenues. Good examples of this are of course Stonehenge, Callanish and the megalithic alignments at Carnac. I firmly believe that Neolithic man employed such layouts as celestial calendars. You must remember that farming was just becoming important as a means of subsistence, having replaced the thousands of years of hunter-gathering. And as any farmer will tell you, expert knowledge of the seasons is crucial for good farming practice.' He glanced over the student's shoulder at the approaching mysterious visitor and a tiny germ of apprehension came into his mind. It was nothing more than the unexpected, he tried to tell himself and yet, some small feeling of unease began to fester inside. Who was this person and, more importantly, what did he want? That rational part of his mind told him that this was perfectly innocent, nothing more than a casual visitor come to take a look at the barrow.

The student, noticing Madden's curiously concerned expression, turned to look at the stranger who was now some hundred yards away.

'Why don't you go and round up the others while I see what he wants.' Madden, like most academics, was not renowned for his social skills, preferring to deal only with university staff and students. Indeed, it was one of the main reasons why he had, from an early age, wanted to be an archaeologist for, in his opinion, the dead were far more interesting and easy to deal with than the living.

Now that the stranger was close it was possible to discern his features and his overall appearance more clearly. He was quite short, his black hair streaked with grey at the temples and styled into a widow's peak, which, together with his pencil-line moustache, leant him an air of peculiarity that bordered on the eccentric. His eyes were of piercing slate-grey and he was very finely dressed; cravat and waistcoat visible under the folds of his raincoat. The knuckles of his right hand were white from grasping the silver, lion-headed cane he had brought with him. There was something about his overall appearance that made Madden think of Victorian theatrical villains — all he was missing was a red-lined cape and a top hat.

'Professor Madden?' called out the stranger.

'Yes, that's me. Can I help you?' Behind him, Madden could hear the sounds of his students mustering, getting ready to head back to the minibus, the field-trip now all but complete. One more barrow and a cursus to visit and then back to the university. All being well they would be back in time for lunch.

'I do hope so. I really do. First, let me introduce myself. My name is Rupert Slythe, and I understand that you're an expert on prehistoric monuments and the like.' He took out a long-stemmed clay pipe and pressed a wad of shredded tobacco into it, lighting it carefully, then blowing out a cloud of pungent blue smoke. 'Forgive me, but I'm completely ignorant of such things. However I do know something that might be very interesting to one such as yourself.'

'And just what's that, Mr. Slythe?' At

the back of Madden's mind he couldn't help but feel that this was a set-up, a prank orchestrated by some of the students. This man was so outlandish, both in appearance and in his overall persona, that there surely had to be something funny going on. His students walked past, heading for the minibus, and he detected some sniggering as they went by. However that could merely have been due to the bizarre look of the visitor, the less suspicious part of his brain tried to tell himself.

Slythe looked to his feet, clearing thinking how to proceed before raising his head to look the professor in the eye. 'Well, you see, I own a large country estate — Farthing Downs Manor, to be precise — '

'I know of it. It's near Cambridge, isn't it?' interrupted Madden.

'That's correct. Anyway, on the grounds of my estate there are several of these so-called barrows and things, as well as one small stone circle.'

Madden nodded. 'Yes, I'm aware of that. The Devil's Ring is the name for that stone circle.'

'Yes, The Devil's Ring.' Slythe smiled

thinly. 'I wonder why these things always seem to possess such names.'

'There's an easy explanation for that. It's called folklore.' Madden adopted his lecturing tone. 'You see, over the course of the last few hundred years many myths and legends have built up around such places. Our ancestors, unable to explain the presence of such anomalies in the landscape — standing stones, ditches, dykes, hill figures and so on — thought that they must have been built with supernatural intervention. You see, it was hard for them to believe they were purely built by men. They're frequently associated with all sorts of pixies, elves and buried treasure — all nonsense, of course. We now know that Neolithic man was incredibly industrious and inventive. Take the bluestones at Stonehenge for example: they were transported some one hundred and fifty miles from South Wales to Wiltshire.'

'Fascinating.' Slythe took a puff on his pipe. 'It would seem that I've come to the right person. You see, only the other day my gamekeeper found one of these standing stone things in the undergrowth, hidden away in a small copse on the edge of my land. And, although I've yet to see it, he informs me that there's some kind of writing on it.'

Madden was interested yet sceptical. 'If there's writing on it you can be certain of one of two things. One, it's not Neolithic, or two, whatever writing is on it must be relatively modern, with the possible exception of Roman graffiti. Is it possible that it's part of some folly built within the last two hundred years? Your gamekeeper could also be getting confused with so-called cup-and-ring markings or decorative whorls and spirals, which along with labyrinth designs have been found on some standing stones. I can assure you however that there won't be — ' He stopped, intrigued, as the other removed a brown envelope from a pocket and took out a slip of paper. 'What's that?'

'These are some of the markings he copied down.' Slythe handed the piece of paper to the professor.

Madden reached into his pocket for his spectacle case and took out his horn-rimmed reading glasses. Putting them on, he looked down at the scrap of paper, eyes widening in confusion and disbelief at what he saw. At first it was just an anarchic conglomeration of meaningless, chaotic symbols, none of which represented any known pictorial image. Crudely linear in disposition, and undoubtedly copied down hastily and poorly, there remained enough to point at some semblance to a rudimentary script rather than but a mere drawing. It was clearly untranslatable, by himself at least, and he doubted whether any of his fellows at the university would be able to understand it. With that thought, the suspicion that this was an elaborate, well-thought-out hoax struck once more.

'Strange, wouldn't you agree?'

'If it's genuine.' Madden handed the piece of paper back to Slythe.

'Of course it's genuine. What makes you think otherwise?'

'The fact that if it is authentic then it turns our understanding of Neolithic life on its head, suggesting that writing, even in such a proto-literate form such as that, existed in this country before the Roman occupation. And besides, why this one stone and no other? What's so special about *it*?'

'That's what I was hoping you'd find out.' Slythe tapped out the burnt contents of his pipe. 'I'd like to invite you and whatever team you require to have a look at this stone. I'm a rich man, Professor Madden, and I'd be more than willing to fund your investigation.'

'I must say I am intrigued.' The mention of private funding certainly sweetened the deal.

'Well whenever's a good time for you. However, could I recommend that you start sooner rather than later. It's not as though it's going to go anywhere, but I'll be travelling to Europe in the New Year. So can we say sometime early next month?'

Madden removed his diary from an inner pocket, consulted it briefly, then said: 'What about if I come over in order to carry out a preliminary examination? Let's say, a week on Thursday, December second.'

'Excellent.'

Together the two men headed back to the car park.

*   *   *

It was a cold and bright winter's morning, the low sunlight throwing long shadows from the trees that lined the main approach to Farthing Downs Manor, making Madden squint in order to drive safely. Accompanying him, in the passenger seat, was Associate Professor Doctor Fred Walker, a tall, lean man with a curly mop of brown hair and a boyish look to his face, despite being in his late fifties.

'I am reminded once again that we must be in the wrong profession,' commented Walker, taking in the expanse of the visible grounds. 'I bet this guy has some money. Just look at the size of this place. It's almost as big as the entire county.'

'Over two and a half thousand acres, I believe,' replied Madden.

'Two and a half thousand acres! Good God! Imagine the potential for doing some field-walking here. I daresay there's a lot that could be found if we were granted permission to undertake some full-scale excavations. I was looking at the aerial photograph you mentioned regarding this place the other day and it's covered in sites — barrows, ditches, dykes, you name it.'

'Yes, but remember we're here to take a look at this standing stone.' Madden was slowing the car down, the huge, rambling manor house now coming into view. 'Once we've got on Mr. Slythe's good side by carrying out this investigation he may let us conduct a full examination of this area.'

They drew up into the large, gravelled car park at the front of the house. Bathed in the stark December sunlight, the three-storey building was grand in scale and opulent in architectural design, and yet it possessed a grim and slightly ominous look. Tall, sombre gables rose on either side of the massive oaken front door; small, leaded windows, half-hidden by the clinging ivy, stared like sightless eyes across the sloping, overgrown lawn; high chimneys like pointing, accusing fingers thrust skyward from the crenellated roof.

Slythe had clearly been awaiting their arrival, for no sooner had the two of them got out of the car than he came striding towards them dressed in what seemed to be the same clothes Madden had seen him wearing on that first occasion.

'Good morning,' Slythe greeted them. 'What a lovely day.'

'Hello.' Madden stretched his arms. It had been a solid two-hour drive and his muscles were feeling rather tense from being stuck behind the wheel for that amount of time. 'Yes, it certainly is a nice morning. May I introduce my friend and associate, Doctor Walker. He too specialises in Neolithic archaeology.'

'Pleased to meet you.' Walker nodded. In one hand he carried a large holdall filled with a collection of tools: trowels, paper for taking rubbings, tape measures, coloured chalks, a geologist's hammer and a camera.

'Excellent.' Slythe beamed. 'Well, gentlemen, I'm sure you're eager to have a look at this thing, so if you'll just follow me around to the shed at the rear we can pick up some tools to assist in doing a bit of clearance. As I told you at the time, Professor Madden, the area where it's located is very overgrown. There are thorns and nettles as well so we should all put on some heavy gloves.'

Together they marched off to the shed to don their gloves and pick up some old-fashioned sickles and a wicked-looking scythe before setting off.

Carrying the scythe, Slythe whistled as he led them out past the rear of the manor, his long shadow making Madden temporarily think of the Grim Reaper. Despite the fact that he no longer entertained the notion that any of this was a hoax, he was confident that it would all turn out be a gross, yet innocent misunderstanding. Yes, there would undoubtedly be a stone somewhere in the dense undergrowth, but he figured it would be but a boulder upon which some vandal had scrawled such gibberish perhaps with the very intention of perplexing prehistorians.

Before them was a shallow valley. Across from them, crowning the opposite rise was a small copse of beech trees, the undergrowth that lay beneath them thick, dark and, from this distance, impenetrable-looking. To Madden's trained eye there seemed to be a strange artificiality to what at first glance he had assumed to be a natural feature. Whether it was due to the way it seemed to conform to the contours of the landscape or something else he didn't know.

'There's the wood,' said Slythe, pointing. 'Just be careful on the slopes. It can be quite treacherous, especially after the rain when it becomes muddy.'

Taking his warning to heart, Madden and Walker carefully descended into the shallow valley bottom before making the uphill trudge. Walker slipped twice, his movements impeded by the holdall he was carrying, but he avoided any serious hurt.

Eventually they reached the top and approached the ring of dark trees.

'Although my gamekeeper cleared a bit of a path into the interior a few days ago, it's still very overgrown, so we'll need to hack some of this vegetation away,' said Slythe. Gripping his scythe, he stared into the thorny barrier before them. 'I think if we start about here where the bramble's less thick.' He made a series of rather ineffectual swipes at the wiry foliage.

Madden nodded to Walker, who rested

his equipment bag on the grass. The two of them then joined Slythe in hacking and chopping their way through the coils of bramble and trailing weeds and thicket. It was hard going, the thorns tearing cruelly at every inch of exposed skin and snagging at their clothing, and on one occasion Slythe came close to accidently severing Walker's hand with a particularly careless swing.

They were all hot and tired after only thirty minutes of work and their progress was slow and painful.

Sweating, Walker turned to Slythe and said: 'Just what the hell was your gamekeeper or whatever he is doing in here in the first place?'

'He — he was looking for his dog. It ran off while he was out here and he heard its barks.'

'And why's he not helping?' There was a tinge of anger in Madden's voice. He was not overly fond of physical labour, preferring to sit in cosy libraries or pontificate about ancient sites from the comfort of the lecture hall. Not that he was adverse to the odd field trip now and then but that didn't involve this intensity of labour — after all, that's what students were for.

'Unfortunately he's had to go home. A sudden family bereavement, I understand. I've given him as much leave as he needs. He's a nice fellow and very good at his job. Besides, if it hadn't been for him and his mangy mutt this thing would've remained undiscovered.' Slythe renewed his savage attack on the jungle-like undergrowth, the broad swings of his scythe now making some inroads.

'I'm getting fed up with this,' cursed Madden. 'If I'd have known it was this bad I'd have got a team of students down to do the clearing.'

'We still could,' replied Walker. 'If we were to get — '

'I can see the stone!' shouted Slythe excitedly. 'Not much more now. See, just through that gap in the trees.' He pointed into the shadowy interior where sunlight dappled and filtered through the leaf-filled tree branches high overhead. 'That must be it.'

Both Madden and Walker peered to

where the other indicated. It was mostly dark and shadow-filled and there still remained a lot of chest-high foliage between them and it, but there was something there, something tall and towering, half-hidden amongst the weeds and warped tree trunks.

Their morale bolstered somewhat by this tantalising glimpse, they set about their difficult task once more. Cursing from numerous stings and grazes, and swinging their tools as though macheteing a path through a jungle they set about fiercely, trailblazing a way forward.

After ten minutes they were rewarded for their not inconsiderable efforts by their first real view of the solitary standing stone. Emerging from the slightly raised ground, half-screened by a gnarled tree trunk and festooned with a net-like mass of weeds and ivy, the stone stood nearly nine feet high. It was by and large irregular in shape yet still maintaining a certain degree of rectangularity to it. Large patches of moss and lichen covered its uppermost part. In many ways it conformed to the usual details of a standing stone, and yet there was a strange feature that immediately caught Madden's eye.

Almost on eye level, what appeared to be a perfect circle, maybe a foot or so in diameter, had been removed from it by means unknown.

'There, gentleman, is your stone.' Slythe gestured towards it, one arm extended.

'This is certainly unusual!' Hacking away the brambles that lay between him and the stone, Madden struggled forward. The circular hole had him truly perplexed and, on nearing and giving it a cursory examination, his initial thought was that it had been drilled straight through.

'Well I've never seen any — ' Walker stopped mid-sentence and looked down as his right boot made an unsavoury-sounding crunch on something. Looking down, he was mildly shocked to see that the ground, under the weeds, was strewn with small bones and animal skeletons. 'God! Look at this.'

Madden's initial excitement now turned to revulsion as he looked down at his feet and saw the dull white scattering of small skulls, femurs and ribcages that were strewn around.

'I wonder what animal did this? A fox, perhaps?' Having no real knowledge of British wildlife it was the best suggestion Walker could offer. 'Anyway, I'll just go back and get the holdall.' He turned and went for the equipment bag.

'It could be foxes,' said Slythe, absently, his eyes fixed instead on the up-thrusting stone with a strange kind of adoration.

Madden returned his attention to the megalith. 'I've never seen anything like this in all my life. This circular hole is most intriguing. It looks almost perfect. Certainly there are similar things, Men-an-Tol in Cornwall and the Long Stone in Gloucestershire, but there's a certain something about this one that has me perplexed.' He waited until Walker had joined them. 'Let's clear the base and scrape some of this lichen off, see if we can find this writing.'

Using their trowels, the two archaeologists scratched at the surface, clearing away the mysterious hump of earth and the animal bones that surrounded the base of the stone. Delicately, they then set about removing the larger patches of moss and lichen. It did not take them long to discover the very faint, indeed almost imperceptible, lines of weird, unrecognisable symbols, which ran in horizontal bands around the stone.

★　★　★

In Slythe's large study, Madden and Walker pored over the rubbings they had made, examining the tiny markings with the aid of powerful magnifying lenses. Neither of them could offer any immediate explanation, each as baffled as the other by the inscriptions. However, Walker was becoming increasingly convinced that it was indeed some form of proto-script, perhaps some runic precursor, whilst Madden remained doubtful.

'Any idea as to what it is?' asked Slythe from where he sat at the end of the table puffing on his pipe, his presence momentarily forgotten by the two experts, such was their level of fascination in their work.

Madden looked up. 'Not as yet. It really is an enigma. Doctor Walker's of the opinion that it might indeed be an as yet unidentified text but I'm not so sure. I think a more detailed epigraphical examination is warranted before we can reach any genuine conclusion.' He straightened his glasses. 'Such petroglyphs can be notoriously hard to interpret clearly.'

'Is it translatable?' asked Slythe.

'Hard to say,' answered Walker. 'If it is indeed some form of incipient language then it's nothing with any known parallels. It could take years to decode. If it is indeed a language.'

Slythe looked disappointed. 'If it is a language surely you'll be able to decipher it sooner than that?'

'I'm afraid not. We've got nothing even remotely contemporary to compare it with. It's clearly not related to Latin so we have to rule that out as a possible contemporary source. We really will be guessing in the dark, I'm afraid.' With a shake of his head, Walker returned his focus to the rubbing before him.

'What about the hole? Does that have

any significance?'

'I daresay those who put it there believed that it did,' answered Madden. 'Such things have been accredited with fertility and recuperative powers. However that's getting into the realm of New Age weirdness.' He shook his head. 'And that's something we always stay well clear of.'

'Yes,' laughed Walker. 'Whatever you do don't mention the druids.'

Half an hour passed, the two scholars becoming more and more agitated in their discussion. One of them would mention some point or other only for the other to instantly dismiss it.

In the end they seemed no closer to any form of conclusive agreement, each as entrenched in their own private view as the other. For whereas Walker had come round to the idea that it was a groundbreaking discovery: the lettering authentic and suggestive of a primordial, pre-Sumerian writing system, Madden was not so easily convinced. For one thing there was no easy means of dating the stone, nor could it be taken as a given that the writing matched the date that the stone was put in position.

'Well there's little more that can be done other than to make an accurate record of this find,' said Madden, resignedly. 'I'll see if anyone in the linguistic department can make anything of this but I'm not hopeful.'

'One more archaeological mystery,' sighed Walker, delicately rolling up the pieces of paper. He then put them in a long cardboard tube for safekeeping.

'I'd like to thank you Mr. Slythe for all of your help,' said Madden. 'And obviously if we do succeed in finding out anything of interest we'll keep you informed.'

★   ★   ★

Madden was in his small office arranging his lecture notes for the new term starting in January. The university was closing down for the Christmas holiday and this was the final day before all of the students went home. It had been a tiring last couple of weeks and consequently he had largely forgotten about Rupert Slythe and the peculiar megalith. After the initial thrill of its discovery and having shown the rubbings to some of his fellow academics — none of whom had been able to make anything out of it — he had tucked them away in a drawer, meaning to return to them at a later date.

The phone on his desk began to ring. He picked it up.

'Professor Madden. It's Rupert Slythe.'

'Ah, Mr. Slythe, how are you?'

'Fine. I'm glad I managed to get through to you. I've been calling your office for the past few days and I was beginning to think that you'd gone on your Christmas break.'

'Today's the last day of term, thank God.'

'Anyway, two things: firstly, I was wondering whether you've had any success in translating the writing on the stone; and secondly, and more importantly, I was wondering if you could come over here, for there's something I'd like you to take a look at. I think it may be important.'

'In answer to your first question, I'm

afraid that I've been unable to make any sense of the inscriptions, nor can anyone else. And as for coming over, well — '

'I do think it's important.'

'Tell me what it is.'

'I can't really describe it but I'm sure it will interest you.'

'Very well. Let me just check when.' Madden consulted his diary. He would be busy over the weekend marking end-of-term essays and it was a good two-hour drive to Farthing Downs Manor. However he was planning to spend Christmas Day at his sister's, so he could combine the two as she lived relatively nearby. 'What about next Friday, Christmas Eve?'

'I'll be out that day, I'm afraid.' Slythe's voice sounded rather sorrowful. 'What about the Tuesday before?'

Madden sighed. 'Very well. I'll see you then.'

*　★　*

During the two-hour drive to Slythe's stately home Madden couldn't get a certain nervousness out of his system. It had started that morning, developing slowly yet surely, the nibbling at his senses now a gnawing at the pit of his stomach, making him feel nauseous.

It was a glorious morning, similar to the day he and Walker had come out here, the low sunlight gilding the trees and dazzling off the road.

Momentarily lost in his own thoughts, he cursed as he missed the turning that led to Farthing Downs Manor. The road was empty so, checking his rear-view mirror, he reversed and was just about to turn into the side road when suddenly a huge flatbed truck laden with cut timbers roared out from it. There was a squeal of breaks and somehow disaster was narrowly avoided. A bearded, irate driver rolled down his window and hurled a torrent of verbal abuse at Madden before speeding off again.

Badly shaken, Madden took several deep breaths, his whole body tingling, the hands that grasped the wheel rigid, the knuckles white. That had been a near thing, and no mistake.

In the distance he could hear the

thundering sound of another approaching truck. He pulled the car into a lay-by and waited until this second, tree-laden lorry had passed. Once he had regained his composure he then pulled into the side road and drove carefully and cautiously towards Slythe's house.

Upon arrival he was greeted by the man himself, his attire the exact same as on their previous meetings.

'Good morning, Professor.'

'Mr. Slythe. I'm pleased to see you again.'

'You look a little tense.'

'Oh, just a close shave back there at the turnoff.'

'One of the timber lorries?'

'Yes. Bloody idiot driver.' Madden combed his hair back.

Slythe removed a silver hipflask from his pocket. 'This might calm your nerves a little.' He offered it to the other.

Madden unscrewed the top and took several hearty sips. It was good whisky. He wiped his mouth dry. 'Anyway, just what is it you want me take a look at?' he asked, handing the hipflask back.

218

'I found a book that might interest you.' Slythe gestured for his guest to make his way inside the house. 'It's in my study.'

'A book? What kind of book?'

'A very old book.'

They entered the house and went into the study.

There were people in there. A dozen or more. People in dark suits.

An aura of sheer confusion threatened to engulf Madden completely. *What was this?*

Sweat popped out on his forehead and he could feel his heart thumping away in his chest. He was feeling dizzy, his vision blurring somewhat. Unsteadily, he lowered himself into a chair. His brain was swimming, his vision now ebbing and flowing in pulsing waves making things look kaleidoscopic. Faces crowded closer. There was a dull throbbing in his head; a pounding in his brain that grew to a booming crescendo. There was cruel-sounding laughter. Then everything went dark and he slumped out of the chair, landing awkwardly on the carpet.

* * *

Slowly, painfully, Madden opened his eyes and a terrifying realisation struck him. His hands were bound tightly with thick cord, as were his feet. He was lying bare-chested on the hard floorboards of an empty garret room, dying sunlight shining in through a high window. A gag had been stuffed into his mouth and there was a terrible taste on his tongue. His head ached.

Raging fear raced through him. Wrenching his aching neck muscles, he tried to turn his head, to see if there was anything in the room that might assist him to escape from this terrible predicament. But there was nothing.

What the hell was going on? It seemed clear to him that Slythe must have drugged him — no doubt something he had slipped into the whisky in the hipflask he had drunk from. The real question was what was the motive behind this abduction and critically, just how was he going to escape? The window was far too small for him to use, so that left the door. But first he would have to try and struggle free.

With difficulty, he managed to slide his thumbs under the thick rag that had been wrapped around his mouth. Then it was just a case of wiggling it back and forth, slackening it so that he managed to pull it free and peel it down over his jaw. The cord around his wrists had been tightly fastened, however, and without a knife — A sudden idea came to him. He doubted whether it would work but given the circumstances it was as good a plan as any.

Rubbing his heels back and forth, he managed to work his right boot off. He shifted his body down, taking a bootlace in his mouth before rolling towards the wall and, using that as a support, he clambered first to his knees and then to his feet, the boot dangling from between his clenched teeth. He gathered the boot into his hands, offered a small prayer of thanks for its sturdiness and then threw it as hard as he could at the window.

It was a poor shot, missing the window by a foot or so.

He had no option but to try again. It was a difficult procedure: bending, retrieving the boot in his mouth and trying to throw it with bound wrists, but mercifully on his fourth attempt the window splintered. On his ninth attempt it cracked and after several more hits it broke, but he lost his boot. What he got in exchange was a scattering of glass shards.

Hoping against hope that the sound of the breaking window would not alert anyone, Madden scurried over to the fragments of window and, taking a shard, began sawing through the bonds at his ankles. He got cut and he got sliced but the need to escape drove him through the pain and soon his legs were free. Now came the hard part.

Wriggling free from his other boot, he then began collecting some of the glass in it. He walked over to the door, and pushed a shard into the door jamb, wincing as it gashed through his thumb. Bright red, coin-sized splats of blood covered the floorboards. Using his boot he tapped the shard in further. He then began cutting, sawing at the cords on his wrists, hoping that the glass was firmly lodged. He was in luck and after a few minutes he cut through the last strands.

'Thank you God,' he muttered. He reached for the door handle and twisted it.

It was firmly locked.

★   ★   ★

Sometime later a key turned in the lock and the door opened. It was opened by a man in a white, hooded robe. In one hand he held a gun. He looked somewhat surprised to see Madden standing before him, believing him to be bound and gagged. There were two more men, dressed similarly, behind him.

'What is this?' asked Madden.

'Just shut up and come with us.' The man gestured with the gun. 'And don't try anything stupid. It's loaded.'

At gunpoint, Madden, bleeding, bootless and bare-chested, was led from the attic room down a long corridor and down a large flight of steps into the main entrance hall of the manor. From a side room he could hear loud talking, and a moment or so later Slythe and three others stepped into view. Slythe was dressed in a sable robe with red trimmings whilst the others were all in white.

'Slythe, you son of a bitch,' Madden snarled.

'Professor Madden,' replied Slythe, casually. 'I'm so pleased you could join us.'

'What is this? Devil-worship? Paganism?'

Slythe smiled slyly. 'Nothing like that. We're all part of an Order that goes much further back. One that believes in the chthonic deities of the Earth. For all your knowledge of ancient sites you remain ignorant of the true connection, don't you? There are things aeon-long buried within the ground that still slumber, waiting for the time when the stars are right and the proper words are chanted so that they can rise once more. Today is the winter solstice, the shortest day, and one of great significance to our Order. And, in a few short hours the sun will set and, well, you'll see.' His smile widened.

'You're mad. You're all insane. You should be locked up.'

Slythe merely shrugged his shoulders. 'If you say so.' With a nod of his head, he gestured to one of his men. 'Get him ready.'

Madden was forced into another room where he was tied to a chair. A man then began to paint red and blue symbols on his bare chest, hands and face. His socks were removed and the bizarre artwork spread to his feet. This was crazy, absolutely unreal, he tried to tell himself. It wasn't happening and yet he knew it was. His head suddenly ached and there were subtle probings in his mind, as if something cold and chill and evil had crept into his brain and was squatting there, tensing every muscle and fibre of his body, willing them to do what it wished. He opened his mouth to scream, but only weird laughter bubbled out. He fought back, desperately, trying to rid himself of whatever it was in his mind.

He was convinced that he was now being ritually prepared in order to be sacrificed, to appease whatever powers presided over this weird, pre-druidic religion that Slythe and his disciples believed in. Oh God, what were they going to do with him? His mind screamed at him, and terror seeped through him in a surging wave, leaving his body exhausted, his spirit spent. How long was this dreadful preparation going to take and how long did he have before these fiends dragged him, kicking and screaming, to their altar?

'Why are you doing this? Let me go.'

The painter never said a word, instead, methodically and intricately, carrying on his task. It took the best part of twenty minutes but eventually it came to an end. Another man then unfastened his bonds.

'Alright, move it.'

The ever-present gun waved before Madden's eyes, compelling him to get to his feet and follow orders. He was forced out into the hall where two more white-robed men waited by the open doors.

Outside it was getting dark, the sun low down.

Gulping down a lump in his throat, Madden staggered forward. Fear was now a tangible knot in his chest, tightening into a black web of panic. His mind kept screaming at him to try to flee from this place. To run while there was still time. Because if he didn't —

A sudden thought came into his head. Yes, they were armed but would they risk shooting him if he was going to be sacrificed? Surely that was a risk they wouldn't take, and yet it was a risk he felt he had to take — the hope that they wouldn't put a bullet in his back.

They were now outside. There were four of them, including one with a gun. All of them were in their white ankle-length robes. He could see many parked cars, all expensive-looking vehicles. This diabolical cult of weirdoes were obviously rich as well as mad.

If he was going to make a break for it he would have to go now.

With a savage cry, he turned and swung his right fist into the face of the man on his left. With some satisfaction he felt the nose burst. He then sped off, his bare feet smacking painfully on the stretch of gravel. Jumping and screaming, he got to the lawn where he picked up his pace, dreading that report from the gun, which would bring everything to an end.

The gunshot never came but a host of threatening yells screamed from behind him. Throwing a quick look over his shoulder he could see his pursuers, their movements thankfully impeded by the long robes they wore.

Madden ran as fast as he had ever run in his life away from the house, away from the madness.

Some hundred yards ahead he could see a row of high hedge.

Behind him, he heard a car engine start up. He looked back once more and his heart sank to see a car bearing down on him, its driver wild-eyed, an insane grin on his face.

He ran on and on, his lungs afire, his heart thumping like a jungle drum. He reached the hedge line and dived, painfully, into the undergrowth. Brambles clawed at his flesh as he fiercely tore his way deeper into the thicket. Nettles stung his feet.

A car door slammed shut. Voices cried out.

It was getting dark and cold. Shadows lengthened.

Savagely, he clawed and crawled deeper

into the thicket. Pain was a raw, screaming thing in his brain. He fell into a weed-covered ditch, his body now spattered with blood and dirt. There were thorns embedded in his back. His skin itched and tingled.

'I see him! He's over here,' a voice rang out.

Madden's heart sank. His tormentors were closing in and he was sure that this time they didn't mean him to slip through their fingers. Then there were more shouts and hooded figures crowded around. He staggered to his feet. Resistance was futile. They had him. His escape attempt had been desperate and short-lived.

★   ★   ★

Mumbling madly, Madden was lashed to the megalith with lengths of rope, his chest pinned against the cold stone, his arms spread wide as though embracing it. His face was pushed into the central hole and then secured, holding him completely immobile. His vision was now tunnelled, his sight limited to the aperture before him. His skin crawled.

The copse of trees and the thick undergrowth he, Walker and Slythe had battled their way through over two weeks ago had now been completely cleared so that the stone stood alone, isolated. From his perverse vantage point, Madden was blinded by the dying rays of the sun as it set, directly before his eyes. It was sinking slowly on the distant horizon and he knew that this stone had been located specifically on a celestial alignment.

The hooded men, thirty or more, gathered in a semi-circle before him. They were chanting quietly.

Slythe broke from their ranks and strode over towards him, a large, strange-looking book in his right hand.

'Why? Why me?' Madden pleaded.

'Why?' Slythe pondered the question for a moment. 'I've many reasons.' He checked his watch and looked out at the setting sun.

'Tell me.'

Slythe turned to face him. 'For over twenty years you've plundered the treasures of countless barrows and grave chambers. You've brought teams of grubby, ignorant imbeciles stomping and destroying many of the ancient monuments. You butcher our holy sites in the pathetic name of science without consideration or veneration, forming erroneous and insulting hypotheses whilst cowering behind your mask of responsibility. You claim you are restoring our heritage but you are not the custodian of the past. *I am!*'

Madden spat his contempt. He was completely helpless — at the mercy of this psychotic, egotistical and merciless man.

Slythe raised the book. 'Within this, our holy tome, is the translation to the words on the stone. In dreams I was informed of the stone's importance and its location. I was informed to find one such as you and to make a clearing in which to gather the faithful. As you can see, I have a considerable following. And our numbers will swell until we cast down the Christian defiler.'

The winter solstice sun was now just a sliver of crimson in the darkness.

Slythe began reading from the book — although the words, if indeed they were words, were alien; hideous grunts and bestial snorts and utterings. The blasphemous sounds slurped and spluttered, filling Madden's tortured mind with obscene images.

And then the sun disappeared and the true madness took a firm hold on him, raging at his mind in one violent burst. Reality broke as the world darkened. A nebulous maelstrom exploded before him and raging fire swept forth. Screaming, Madden saw Slythe falter in his chanting, the look of triumph changing to fear. The fire flowed over and around Madden but did not burn him. Instead, the conflagration raced towards the gathered men.

Through the hole, Madden saw Slythe and his followers consumed and reduced to burning skeletons before his eyes, their blackened bones suspended in mid-air for a moment before collapsing to the ground.

Madden's scream died away as energy flowed into him from the stone, healing his wounds, purging the remains of the drug and even, though he did not know it, returning his grey hair to the light brown colour of his youth. For the stone had once more fulfilled its purpose of prolonging the life and health of its priest at the cost of its willing devotees. This fundamental misunderstanding of the magic involved had resulted in Slythe and his followers paying the ultimate price for their ignorance.

Madden's bonds fell away and he gazed, unbelievingly, at the charred remains around him. He felt better than he had for the past twenty years, the coldness of the December dusk invigorating him. He placed his hands on the stone as the megalith blazed power into its newest priest.

THE END